The Dingle War is about as far-out a war story as you'll ever find, but then, Dingle is about as far out on Ireland's coast as you can find yourself.

While it is true that war is hell, it is equally true that hell hath no fury like an Irishman who's gotten wind of an injustice. And thus, *The Dingle War.*

The hilarity begins when out of this misty, whiskey-steeped peninsula strides twenty-year-old Devin Ryan, and rolls on and on until Devin has single-handedly mastered England, Germany *and* the Vatican!

It's the funniest story to come out of World War II—and you'll agree if you can stop laughing long enough!

The Dingle War

BY BOB DAVIS

PAPERBACK LIBRARY

New York

PAPERBACK LIBRARY EDITION
First Printing: June, 1969

Library of Congress Catalog Card Number: 68-16320

TO MY PARENTS

This Paperback Library Edition is published by arrangement with Prentice-Hall, Inc.

Paperback Library is a division of Coronet Communications, Inc. Its trademark, consisting of the words "Paperback Library" accompanied by an open book, is registered in the United States Patent Office. Coronet Communications, Inc., 315 Park Avenue South, New York, N.Y. 10010.

ONE

My brother, Devin, was called the Dingle wild man. I have no idea what he is called today, but his last correspondence was postmarked Las Vegas. This leads me to believe he is still exchanging coins in the coy, shadowy way which almost plunged Ireland into World War Two—and not on the side of our former overlords, the English. But Devin has been away from the Kerry coast since the fall of 1942; I do not think he would mind if I told of his Dingle affairs. As I look back on his bittersweet deals, my spine stiffens and a cold dampness floods into my palms. The fact is that Devin was the first real entrepreneur and perhaps the last ever to sweep through our little coastal community. Even today, Devin's story is told and retold in the local whiskeries and his critics secretly wish he would come swaggering back with another bombastic plan to enhance their wealth.

I suppose this longing for Devin is an outgrowth of peninsula life—in some ways, a barren, hopeless kind of existence. The Dingle Peninsula darts out into the Atlantic on the southwest tip of County Kerry. All year the Atlantic pounds against the rich green headlands. Above, blue-black clouds race off the sea to land their moisture on the mountains and walled meadows. When the rain stops the mist comes, and when that blows inland, more rain clouds assemble to continue the eternal downpour. This has a dampening effect on the spirits, and people seem bent and defeated by the soft sod and the thick wet air.

Nevertheless, Dingle is a magnificent spot of earth, rugged, breath-taking, forceful in the way it bucks the sea. The rest of Ireland seems hewn down, gentler by comparison. Dingle is sensational. That is the one word which indexes this land. Mountains tilt down to the sea, partitioned off by stone walls as if they were about to collapse

5

into the raging waters. Nothing is moderate here. People are hard. Houses are built ruggedly to stand the gales, and the road curves around the border of the sea like a stiff black ribbon.

The town of Dingle is set along a natural, deep-water harbour. A greyness prevails and some people say the place would be colourful if it were not for the ashen canopy in the sky. Almost every establishment in Dingle is licensed to sell wines and spirits, the establishments being shoe and boot shops, bakery, meat shops and all the rest. In 1939 there was one drinking house for every twenty-one people. This is a handy way of doing things because one can take a whiskey while he buys a bolt or a lager while trying on a new pair of sod boots. The largest and finest structure in town is the church and the parochial life of the community is headed by Father Dunn and a younger curate, one Father Callahan.

Now much has been written about Irish people—their built-in wit, imagination, knotted fists, brawling, laments and the rest. It is enough to say that those of Dingle are just plain rural people, decent and civil, none of whom talk or act like Barry Fitzgerald or Mike Quill. (I once heard the latter speaking out on Telefis Eireann against "bossism".)

But the Dingle people do carry on a dull struggle for existence; that, no doubt, opened the way for the imaginative, mercantile schemes of my brother who poured out his creative energies in a fashion, as I said, never before realised along this coast. I must admit that our family's life in Dingle was separated from the rest of the people. First of all, we lived in a fine two-storey house of brick with central heating, the latter being rare in Ireland and a real wonder along our poor Kerry peninsula.

There was little to separate Devin from any other Irish boy during his early teens (except that he was rich). We were raised primarily by Uncle Shemas, a big, laughing sort of man, who took over the creameries when our father died. He promised the local curate that he would watch after us and mould our lives along true Christian lines. There was some doubt in the priest's mind since our family lived high on the hog and this, according to strict

Irish parochialism, always implied a race after worldliness rather than heavenly mileage. It was not that Father Dunn disliked Uncle Shemas. I recall the curate was our dinner guest on many Sundays, especially bitter cold Sundays when our house was dry and warm.

"Can I heat it up a bit for you, Father?" Uncle Shemas would ask.

Father Dunn thought a bit and, perhaps, just to let Uncle Shemas play with his rheostat, he used to say, "Well, it might be a bit warmer now that I think of it."

Uncle Shemas would then spring for the dial and turn the magic warmth up to a blistering seventy-eight degrees. The air vents poured out the heat until Father Dunn was sweating around his starched Roman collar.

"Could you turn the heat down?" the priest always said and my uncle would respond, taking his stance before the dial on the dining room wall.

I do not think central heating alone caused Devin to embark on his infamous deeds. Some blame must rest with two American periodicals—*The New Yorker*, and a magazine which I have not seen for many years called *Country Gentleman*. These periodicals came to our house after Devin and Uncle Shemas went to Dublin for a weekend in 1937. At the Shelbourne, Devin's eyes popped wide as he thumbed through the slick pages. *Country Gentleman* showed, supposedly, that American farmers were gentlemen of the sod being dressed in tailored clothes and forever posing beside shiny mechanised equipment, none of which bore traces of the fields they were built to plough. The other magazine, dealing with urban life in the "real", cranked up Devin's curious little mind to such an extent that he came back to Dingle saying that something was acutely wrong with our way of life. I cannot understand how *The New Yorker* magazine was supposed to cure the ills of a poor Irish community, but Devin, at least, thought it could, and he sent in a few pounds to subscribe to both journals. A few months later these magazines trickled into our house via the post, and I must say we all took to reading them. Devin not only read them, every last word, but he studied their context and thought that the *Country Gentleman* articles could revolu-

7

tionise our peninsula. Devin continually tore out articles and showed them to our local farmers.

"See," Devin said, "this is what you can do with the proper soil for carrots." But carrot production in New Jersey did not, somehow, settle the Dingle problems.

Then, "Look at this one," Devin said with a gleam in his eyes. "Why can't we raise turkeys for Thanksgiving?" Of course, no one understood Thanksgiving and the idea of raising Irish turkeys for an American holiday did not appear sensible to the shrewder Dingle farmers.

And I remember so well through those aching Irish teas, which ran from the sun's weakening point until it blushed red and died, how Devin would discuss the *Country Gentleman* articles with Uncle Shemas. There was one particularly sharp discord I recall and it had to do with celery. In one of Uncle Shemas's few outbursts, he bellowed,

"Devin, if you do not agree with the writer's advice on celery production, send him a correspondence and say that Devin Ryan, Irish boy agricultural wizard, age eighteen, claims that he knows more than the American editors!"

"I'll be doin' just that," Devin answered sharply, his black, hawkey eyes popping about from side to side as if they had come loose.

Of course, I must admit one thing to be fair and that was Devin's ability to grasp a subject from vocabulary alone when he did not fully understand the nature of the material. Years before, when we were playing in the back room, Devin found several volumes on vegetable production. Now this was, as I remember, just after he learned to read at the national school which might have been in his sixth or seventh year. It was raining that Saturday—oh, I believe it rained every Saturday of our youth—and Devin came upon the dusty vegetable books. He picked them up and, to impress me, began reading the words not knowing what they meant.

So Devin's entry into the world of words and ideas did not come from the usual association of Camelot, kings and fairy princesses; instead, his earliest imagination and recollections centred, quite tragically, upon Brussels sprouts and radishes. And when Uncle Shemas came into

8

our room at half-eight for our bedtime tale, I listened to another chapter of *Treasure Island* but Devin asked for the further developments of long-row carrot planting.

This was, perhaps, our first indication that something might have been going wrong with Devin. Of course, we were not really alarmed, but often Uncle Shemas would pass me a remark since I was the oldest son.

"Isn't it interesting how your brother loves vegetable growing?"

"Yes, it is," I would answer each time. "But why do you suppose, Uncle Shemas, that we cannot get Devin to run a small kitchen garden to the back of the house?"

"We must face the facts, Billy. Devin hates dirt."

"But how can you grow up to be a vegetable expert and hate dirt?"

And so often I would look into the big face of my uncle and we would exchange a sort of wonderment, each of us shrugging our shoulders. In those years it was exciting growing up with the mystery of Devin surrounding us like a coiled spring. (It was *years* before his little twists of fancy took on a petrifying nature.)

The first small fright we experienced, perhaps the initial portent, was the day Uncle Shemas came running into the house at half-two. I knew this was most unusual because our uncle stayed about his creameries until just before tea time.

"Billy, I feel trouble," Uncle Shemas said, blowing out long breaths. "I was coming along by the Ventry Road and there was a small group of men gathered by the stone wall. I stopped, of course, to see the trouble. Well, my God, there in the middle of this group, sitting there with a cigarette smoking away like a volcano, was your brother Devin."

Uncle Shemas paused for a breath and I tried to soften the blow, but it turned out to be the wrong blow.

"We both know Devin takes a fag now and then."

"Fag! Fag! What do I care whether he smokes his bloody head off. Your brother, the Brussels sprouts expert, was announcing to the farmers that he had just been appointed a District Commissioner by the Minister of Agriculture in Dublin."

"How could they believe it?"

"I don't know, but the farmers were asking him questions on vegetable production and, the saints be praised, your brother was carrying on like an expert, like Jesus in the Temple at twelve."

"How did he act when he saw you?"

"Didn't disrupt him in the least," Uncle Shemas cried, "now can you get over that? Devin has appointed himself a District Commissioner. I hope Father Dunn is ready in the confessional."

After Devin became the District Commissioner, we thought it best never to mention the self-appointment at our dinner table even though poor Uncle Shemas was congratulated on the success of his nephew. This led the man to wear a *continual mask* of uneasiness.

It was, perhaps, six months after the celery argument that Devin announced to Uncle Shemas one day, "That man on *Country Gentleman* was wrong about the celery."

"And did you write him, Devin?"

"That I did, but they never published my communication."

"And I suppose you wrote it in your scratchy hand on that cheap paper you use for school problems?"

"Indeed I did," Devin answered, not realising the point of the inquiry.

"And you addressed your correspondence to the Vegetable Editor?"

"Yes," Devin answered weakly.

Uncle Shemas got up and meandered about the room looking towards the wet, green mountains in the distance. He turned and moved his sweet face towards Devin's.

"My boy, I know you have become an expert on vegetables and you have achieved this yourself, but let me tell you something which might change the whole course of your life."

(If Uncle Shemas, God bless his soul, only knew what profound national consequences his next few sentences would have upon the world and Devin Ryan, I am certain he might have taken the easier way and remained quite mute.)

"I always say," continued Uncle Shemas, "go directly to the top; speak to the head man for results. More time is wasted in this world because people are too timid to take their problems and opinions to the very head person. Now, when you go to mass, aren't you speaking *directly* to God, the head person? We don't have to take our case to St. Patrick first. Of course, that would be fine, but there is no divine protocol. So, Devin, you made a mistake in writing to the Vegetable Editor. Write to the Editor-in-Chief, and you must do it on fine paper and not in that poor hand of yours. Appearance counts!"

Devin did not comment on Uncle Shemas's lecture that evening, but as we were taking our Limerick bacon in the next morning, he said, "You're right, Uncle Shemas. Would you consider buying me a typewriter if I learned how to use it? I could type your bills and in that way pay back the expense."

Uncle Shemas beamed with pride. It was the first time that Devin had paid the older man the least compliment, and it seemed to arouse something deep within him as if Devin, for that moment alone, were his son.

A fortnight from then, we cranked up the old Austin and rode into Killarney for what Uncle Shemas said was a surprise. We took a large meal with sherry and wine at the hotel and then went to the local printing shop where Uncle Shemas handed each of us a wrapped cardboard box. Devin tore into his and yanked out a sheet of fine rag stationery with his name engraved on the top.

(So as not to favour Devin, Uncle Shemas had my name inscribed on a letterhead also, but I never took to writing since I was not in the least upset by such worldly topics as celery growing.) But Devin's eyes grew wider and he gleamed with a boyish pride as he held the paper to the light looking for the watermark. And then he discovered the envelopes which said,

> Devin H. C. Ryan, Esq.
> Dunratty House
> Dingle
> County Kerry, Ireland

(And that was an address which would bring on some terror; I am certain that the local Killarney printer had little notion that he was inscribing the letters for terrible deeds to come. But, then, how was any of us to know what things ran around the mind of our little celery expert, God bless him!)

From the print shop we marched behind Uncle Shemas to a hardgoods store where two larger boxes awaited us. Devin was the first one into the packing and as Uncle Shemas stood back glowing, Devin held up a new typewriter.

"It's beautiful, Uncle Shemas," Devin said. "I'll learn to use it very well. I'll become the best typist on the peninsula and I won't type a word on the new writing paper until I am an expert." My own gift was an adding machine and I pretended to be as delighted as Devin, but I could hardly imagine what numbers I was to add.

During the next few months our house was filled with clattering, rattling and clicking and the noise became faster and louder until I suppose Uncle Shemas must have regretted his gifts. I added up the numbers in the national telephone book and Devin became a rather proficient typist taking a self-study course from several books which told one how to be a secretary. Of course, we were all anxious to see the first letter Devin wrote and it went quite naturally, to the Editor-in-Chief of *County Gentleman*. I must admit it was nicely typed with not one strike-over or smudge. Down at the bottom Devin typed in my initials after those of his own as if I were his secretary.

We waited.

Three months later, Devin's letter was printed in *Country Gentleman* and the editors added this comment:

"The editors are pleased to print the following letter received from one of our Irish readers who is a celery expert and local commissioner for agricultural matters."

Uncle Shemas said, "Don't you see, Devin? Isn't it true? Go to the top with a well-presented case and you will get results."

Uncle Shemas was so pleased to see Devin's letter in print that he was not in the least outraged that his young nephew had taken it upon himself to be the local commissioner for agriculture. But I suppose, in a way, Devin was the local commissioner, in spirit anyhow; no one else, including the people from Dublin, knew as much as my brother of local farm matters. The printed letter in *Country Gentleman*, unfortunately, opened up an entire new world to Devin—it was a powerful tool, a weapon, a device. A voice had been invented for my brother which I am sure he is using to this day. At a very young age, Devin learned the arts of correspondence and the airs of importance and he went on unabashed, probably to see how far his letters would take him.

After the *Country Gentleman* success, he wrote a lengthy correspondence to the president of the International Harvester Company saying, in fact, that he was in charge of agricultural reform for the *entire* county. He went on explaining the soil, our creamery operation, the lack of price supports from the government and the nineteenth-century farm methods. Devin did come up with one rather profound conclusion when he wrote,

> . . . my survey suggests one basic problem. We cannot produce enough in volume for the farmer to increase his yield and, thus, return a fair profit for his industry. Representing three hundred thousand farmers as I do, I have been authorised to contact you because of your world-wide reputation in farm matters, with the

end in view of submitting to us a plan which could enrich our production and give this part of Ireland a chance to compete in the world produce markets.

Sincerely,
Devin H. C. Ryan, Esq.
Chairman, Agricultural
Reform Unit
County Kerry and
Peninsula

This sort of letter was a f
Harvester Company and th
well-dressed salesmen sho

hired motor cars. I can remember the white veil of surprise which dropped across their faces when they confronted Devin, the teenage farm reformer. But my brother played the game as a young genius. And using phrases from *Country Gentleman*, he boldly ordered a survey and ended the meeting by saying, "Gentlemen, you have the opportunity to bring Ireland into the twentieth century." Perhaps it was Devin's deep black eyes and his leading chin wrapped with determination that eased the smirks from the hardened salesmen. Their leader got up and announced, "We shall try."

And, indeed, they did.

Five weeks later they submitted a forty-page report on Dingle farm yields, prognostic yields and entry into the foreign market, all, of course, advanced by shiny mechanised equipment from the American manufacturer. Devin called all the leaders of the farm community into the "Bee" pub one Saturday night and gave them a thrashing for their decadent methods.

. . . and do you want new motor cars, washing machines, central heating, wireless sets, electrics stoves? Are these the things you want, just like the American people, your relatives across the plain of water? If you don't want them, you *should* want them. Ah yes, the way to get these refinements of life, my fellow farmers, is by greater yields from the land. We are only held back by lack of equipment. I will propose to the President of Ireland and to the Minister of Agriculture a plan, and I ask you to assist me in signing a petition for government help. The American government pays for everything; why not the Irish government?

While the Dingle farmers were not interested in raising American market or owning electric mechanised equipment and government with joy. Two weeks later Devin posed his three hundred thousand the Minister of Agriculture. He Devin fifty reasons why it was e of them—and finally offered my brother functionary employment.

"I would not take your pittance job! I'll show you! Our goods can be marketed for five times the price we're getting."

Devin returned. They all laughed at my brother. But he went on sticking his long skinny nose into *The New Yorker* or cutting out their jokes and pasting them to pub walls. (Most of the cartoons were not understood by the average Dingleman.)

When Father Dunn came to dinner and saw the collection of American magazines—by this time, they included *Time, Life, Fortune* and *Women's Wear Daily,* the last of which got into Devin's subscription by mistake—he took Uncle Shemas aside quietly telling the man that Devin was devil-bound. My brother went right on and I say, without disrespect for our national school system, that Devin's higher education and much of his worldliness originated from the pages of American periodicals.

TWO

Now, the hate Ireland supposedly has for the British has been mollified and, in most cases, extinguished during recent years. In 1939, though, there were many who still remembered the horror of Easter Week and the painful tyranny enforced by many years of English rule. Personally, I never liked or disliked the English. They bought our produce, paid their bills and, as far as I am concerned, they are reasonable people. Devin's attitude was slightly contrary. And I would say it sprang from our home life and the false worshipping of family heroes. Grandfather Jim was ripped in half by a British machine gun in Dublin and our father died in an attack on the northern border during the summer of 1935.

I do not think one meal passed without some babbled tales of British brutality and opportunism. After years of this, it was obvious that Uncle Shemas was out of stories, but he made up fantasies to satisfy Devin. As we grew, the stories became bolder and bolder; by the time of our late teens, Uncle Shemas's imagination had flown so high that one night he announced with his grave look the "true" facts behind the mass hanging at Dublin's Kilmainham prison.

"Why, do you know," he said, "that the English hung over two thousand Irishmen just for being Irish!"

I doubt whether Devin really believed this; nevertheless, it was the sort of sadistic adventure which fell warmly upon my brother's ears.

"And we must always honour our dead in this house," Uncle Shemas would cry. "Your father and his father died for our freedom. We won the war; now we must fight for the peace." (I never did know what that saying meant.)

Truthfully, it must be admitted that our father did not die before an English gun. It happened that he was off on a Dublin holiday and one night, at the "Brazen Head" pub, he took to drinking too many lagers with some friends. At two in the morning they decided to raid a British barracks beyond the border. Two or three old rifles were rounded up. I cannot understand how they thought they could overcome the English and liberate the whole of Ireland with three guns, but that was the plan of attack. They drove north from Dublin, and at Ulster frontier an armed British soldier poked his head inside the motor car window. My father looked at him and dropped dead of a heart attack. Of course, the story travelled back to the Dingle peninsula with some embellishment and I remember it was said that he gave his life for Ireland in a bitterly fought border contest. (The true story was only revealed one night when Uncle Shemas became drunk at the Dingle "Bee" and promised an attack on Ulster to avenge the death of his brother.)

Uncle Shemas himself keeled over a row of milk cans in the cooling room of the creamery one morning; I am sure he passed on without pain. This was in Devin's nineteenth year. After the will was probated in Killarney, we found ourselves with nine creameries—they were actually cream separating stations—and four thousand pounds.

The day we returned to the empty house at Dingle, Devin called a meeting in Uncle Shemas's study.

"Billy," he started seriously with a ruffled brow, "I know you're the elder, but I'm willing to forget that. What are your intentions?"

I suddenly realised that Devin was sitting behind the desk and I was in front of the desk. My brother had quickly grabbed the seat of supremacy as I knew he would.

"I suppose I'll continue to run the creameries like Uncle Shemas."

"You propose to run the creameries as Uncle Shemas did!" Devin said, sitting back and twirling in his seat. Just at that point the young boy brought out a cigar and looked towards the ceiling as he lit it. "That's interesting," he said after a deep, thinking kind of pause. "You don't plan to improve the operation, or expand, or develop the business in our family name. Interesting, Billy. The very complacency of the peninsula has defeated you at twenty years of age."

"What would you have, Devin?" I said with a blast on my voice.

"I would move, Billy, my dear brother—expand, kick out the old methods and turn this peninsula into an important centre of commerce."

I simply wrapped a smile around my face and nodded yes. He dismissed me, saying that he was working on part two of his agricultural reform program and that I would be quite impressed by his new study. I nodded yes again and departed the room. At that time, I envisioned that we would lose our creamery business along with the inheritance.

Part two of Devin's agricultural reform measures was drafted quickly and we went off to present the ideas to the Minister of Agriculture who was now thinking that a certain black-haired, wild liberal was disturbing the peace of the Kerry countryside. I must say, though, that Devin's new approach was more practical and to the point. He seized upon the basic problem of the dairy industry.

17

Our creameries were only working at forty percent of their two thousand gallon capacity. This, according to Devin, was attributable to haulage problems. (Ireland is one of the few countries in the world where the farmer hauls his own milk to the separating stations.) This is usually accomplished by donkey carts, the farmers lining up their carts twice a week at the stations. This social gathering carves many hours from their work schedules, besides introducing unsanitary conditions around the separators.)

My brother wanted simply to mechanise Irish milk haulage. I agreed with this and accompanied him to the Ministry of Agriculture in Dublin. We marched into the Minister's office and Devin, wearing a new three-piece suit, placed his report on the man's desk with the words, "I'm not taking any more of your government foam, sir. It's time for action. And you had better pay attention to what I am saying because the hope of this bleak, bogged down country rests within the confines of my little skull."

The Minister sat back aghast and I noticed the slightest tremble as he opened the neatly typed report. After a few preambles, Devin stood up commandingly.

"We want a government loan to buy three vans for milk haulage. We will also use these to haul our produce into market."

"Mr. Ryan, we cannot approve this sort of loan. There isn't money to buy vans for every farmer in Ireland."

"Are you saying no? Is that the drift of your words?"

"It is," the Minister retorted.

"Then let me tell you something, sir. I shall have you sacked from your job straightaway! I will mechanise Dingle despite your apathy, the apathy of our farmers and the rest of this wet country!"

Devin turned and marched from the Minister's office. I ran behind, hoping we would not receive a fast inkwell at the base of our necks. My brother had a magical way of returning to normal after the most heated discords. He continued out onto Kildare Street with more brightness and colour in his face than I had ever seen. Devin was like that.

18

THREE

My brother became silent during the fortnight. He was
thinking. Devin returned from his silence with a new plan.
This time he prepared a correspondence to Henry Ford
advising the American industrialist of our problems and
asking him for three Ford vans on a long term loan basis.
Devin said that he was representing four hundred thousand farmers who needed mechanisation and that he was
willing to try out three vans with the possibility of ordering up to sixty thousand. I wonder now how Henry Ford
reacted to this communication—whether he thought
Devin was a complete fool or an Irish leprechaun placing
his imagination on paper. At any rate, a bank representative called upon us in Dingle saying that the Ford Motor
Car Company had asked them to run a check on Devin
Ryan. Devin rose to his finest form, taking the bank
gentleman to our creameries and, then, to nine others
which we did not own. (Of course, he claimed ownership
of every station.)

"You see, sir, I am going to revolutionise the peninsula."

Coming from a frail teenager, this seemed improbable;
but Devin had a way with him and he presented a powerful front to those with whom he talked. This correspondence was received from Henry Ford several weeks later:

Dear Mr. Ryan:
Thank you for your inspiring letter announcing
your plans to mechanize Irish agriculture. Of course, we
are in the mechanization business as you know, but
aside from that, I feel that you possess farsighted ideas.

19

I, too, had these sorts of ideas when I built the first Ford motor car. I must congratulate you on your efforts. Our bank correspondents in Dublin wrote a good report on your business operation, noting particularly your energy and your youth.

I am happy to tell you that I have personally called our manager of the truck division and we are presently preparing three specially painted "Kelly Green" stake trucks with the lettering: THE RYAN BROTHERS, DINGLE, COUNTY KERRY. These will be sent by ship and are to arrive at Galway City within the month. The financing arrangements will be forthcoming from our bankers in Dublin.

I look forward to a report on our stake trucks and, at the same time, congratulate you on your courage and determination. As you know, American industry is propelled by many of your fellow countrymen and I say, with no undue pride, that part of their success in our democracy is due to products from the Ford Motor Car Company.

Sincerely,
Henry Ford, Sr.

The arrival of the letter from Henry Ford and the industrialist's offer to send us three vans brought out in my dear brother a new edge of authority; his head was held higher and he walked about Dingle with a strut. People said, "Good morning, Mr. Ryan." He had become Mr. Ryan while I was still called Billy, as I am to this day. Devin felt, at that point, that his powers of persuasion and evaluation were almost god-like and I remember the morning at breakfast as we were taking our tea, he announced:

"Billy, I'm worried."

"What about, Devin?"

"The international situation."

He threw a clump of papers in front of me. (Each morning we received old editions of *The New York Times* and *The Times* from London plus the Dublin dailies.)

"Look at the headlines," Devin said.

Menacing words were beginning to creep across front pages in those last months of the thirties and the situation in Germany was indeed dark.

"You see, Billy, business is always controlled by the international situation. We don't want to expand in the wrong direction. If there's going to be war, we want to be in the right business position."

That afternoon Devin pasted the headlines all over the kitchen walls and late into the night he marched up and down with the newspaper articles saying to himself, "I'll never last; I'll never last." Then I heard his typewriter clicking out what, even to my ears, seemed to be a message of importance. That next morning he showed me the correspondence and I could hardly conceal my shock and shortness of breath.

My brother who was not yet into his twenties had composed and typed out with all seriousness the following message to a well-known political leader in Germany:

Mr. Adolf Hitler
Reichsführer
The Reich Chancellery
Berlin, Germany

Dear Mr. Hitler:

You do not know me but I am an agricultural leader in Ireland and a friend of Henry Ford, the capitalist. Mr. Ford and I are attempting to revolutionise Irish agriculture by mechanisation. I have taken my funds and placed them into several large purchases of motor vans. I understand that you have spoken often about the necessity for the German farmer to improve his yield with modern methods so we agree on that point at least.

I have been reading newspapers lately and some stories suggest that Germany is angered at her neighbours to the point of going to war. I hope you will not think that I am prying into your personal business and that of your country, but I would like to know if you plan any immediate attacks so that we can know how to gauge the expansion of our company.

Please understand that we are neutral and have no involvement in European affairs, but knowing what is going to happen slightly before it happens, I am sure you will agree, gives one some advantage over the competition. I will keep your answer to my letter in the strictest confidence.

Thank you.

Sincerely,
Devin H. C. Ryan Esq.
District Agricultural Commissioner

"Devin, you are crackers," I said with a small shake coming upon my hand.

"Do you think he will answer?"

"No!"

I was wrong.

Two weeks later an official communication arrived bearing an ominous black eagle in the corner. We sat in Uncle Shemas's study looking at the envelope resting on the cherry wood desk. It was a menacing sight and even Devin, I believe, was slightly amazed to see the official German answer.

"It's probably a form letter reply," he said slowly.

"I don't know, Devin. But it's risky writing to a man like Hitler."

"But didn't Uncle Shemas say go to the top for the answers?"

"But I don't think he meant Hitler."

"Should we have a nip. . . . I mean, while we open the thing?" Devin said.

"We should."

Devin went to the Queen Anne sideboard and handed down a bottle of Jameson and that was the morning we had our first drink before half-eleven, which in Ireland is called the "all right" hour. We sat down gathering our courage and then Devin picked up the envelope and said, "I'm sure, Billy, that Hitler doesn't sit around getting the courage to open *his* mail."

"But we need a boost."

Devin took our ivory-handled opener and sliced

through the edge of the envelope. As he opened the paper, it crackled as all heavy handmade stocks do and up in the corner was a swastika and under it the terrifying title: THE REICHSFUHRER.

I leaned over Devin's shoulder and we read the very words that might change the course of the world.

My Dear Mr. Commissioner:

How nice of you to write from your busy agricultural office in Ireland to inquire whether my country is planning aggressive moves against her neighbours. As you know, I am only the voice of the German people who have traditionally wanted peace with the world. It is right that you should ask me if the hope of the world and the peace of Europe is at stake. It is men like you and millions of other good and peaceful farmers who lose in a time of war.

I can assure you that Germany desires peace and we are meeting in Munich shortly with the British Prime Minister, Mr. Chamberlain, to restress our desire for harmony within the European community. I would advise you to proceed with your expansion plans and not become unsettled with the world situation. We both know that anxious newspapers and political troublemakers have a way of spreading lies. I would say that Germany is leading the cause of peace but we shall have to watch England. Your country has had certain unpleasant relations with the British but I hope these people can be quieted by the good counsel of Mr. Chamberlain.

I take this opportunity to send the affectionate greetings of the German farmers to the hard-working Irish farmers with the hope that all of us will enjoy years of peaceful productivity from the land. Please do not hesitate to write me again on any matter and if you are passing by Berlin someday, stop in to see me.

> Yours in lasting peace,
> Adolf Hitler
> Reichsführer.

I said in those moments a small prayer to Uncle Shemas asking him to guide us, and realised that Devin was only trying to further the economic aims of the peninsula.

And day to day, Devin grew in vocabulary. He had a way of reading three magazines on financial affairs, then starting to talk like an executive. One magazine, *Fortune*, I believe it was, published an article on executive blood pressure. It told about the plight of tired executives and how they should exercise and watch the pressure of the blood. Before reading the article, Devin had not the slightest idea what blood pressure was or the executive art of feeling tired; after reading the article, he believed that feeling tired and strained with slightly high blood pressure was the mark of executive effectiveness. And he no sooner put down the magazine than he said to me,

"Billy, I'm tired. *Very tired.* I think I'll have a check-up."

He went to Doctor Kilmartin the following day complaining of high blood pressure. Devin returned about half-eleven and slumped behind his desk saying dully, "Doctor Kilmartin says I must relax more."

"Do you have high blood pressure?" I asked.

"No," Devin said despondently, "but it could happen at any time. The doctor said I must be on my guard."

It was just a week after the doctor's visit that Devin took out life insurance on himself.

"Billy, if anything happens to me, I want this company to go on. The most important asset we have is my health so don't let anyone upset me. I must *not* be upset. That will be the rule of our corporation. No one is to upset the president. He might fall dead away of a heart seizure any moment."

I wondered about that since Devin was only into his third year of shaving. But my brother had a way of believing the fancies of his mind; he made them come alive with clearness and so we lived in an unreal world where every imagination was herded into hard reality by my dear brother. (Indeed, it was a world which all of us need from time to time, and not to have a bit of a Devin Ryan is not to live.)

24

FOUR

The green vans came into Galway as promised and we rushed up there on the coach with Ronnie Downs, a big brute of a man with a flourishing crop of thick cinnamon hair. He was our creamery foreman and one who could drive any sort of van—so he told us.

They were beautiful—shiny, full of chrome—and, I must say, better than any English van we had seen. We started down to Dingle after clearing customs, with Devin leading the way. What pride I had that bright morning driving the new van with our names lettered upon the sides. I imagined in my daydreams that someday we would have a hundred of these vehicles rolling over every inch of Ireland, and the Ryan Brothers would take over the country's haulage problems. It was on this winding and slow trip through Clare that I began to feel proud being related, as I was, to Devin. And I laughed out loud thinking that it all started because of a few magazines. I suppose that great men must be inspired by something, usually their fathers or a teacher, but here we were—the mechanised Ryan Brothers—reaching new heights all because of some American periodicals. Then again, I figured if it were not for *Country Gentleman* Devin would have been triggered by some other force; but I could not imagine the nature of that force.

My mind was not upon the road or what was happening beyond the second van. Suddenly there was a crash; a cloud of dust puffed up over the stone wall which rimmed the narrow road. I slammed my foot pedal and over the squeak of brakes, there was a crash of bottles which, I am sure, could be heard all the way to Limerick. My van spun around, coming to a stop on the side of the road where

Ronnie's was resting. This cleared the way for me to see Devin's lead vehicle perched over the hip of a wall, the front wheels spinning, hanging in air. Devin darted out and came racing back across the scattered line. I was out, too, to see a very old whiskey van on its side in the wet pasture. The figure pulling himself from the wreckage was a slight man with an outsized nose. A single line of deep red criss-crossed his face beginning just under the front strands of his hair and running to the bumps of his cheekbones. He stood there dazed.

Devin was raging as he tore over the spongy meadow towards this poor bedevilled fellow. There was no doubt that the whiskey driver was in the wrong, besides the fact that he was obviously sampling the cargo enroute. And if Devin had demolished him, he would have had my sympathies. Quite suddenly, Devin eased his gait; finally, he stopped about six feet from the wobbly driver. I do not believe to this day that Devin was studying the man before him, deciding which punch to pull. Instead, to my way of thinking, Devin was wondering about himself. He seemed to understand that the course of this situation—his reaction to the old teamster—would very much decide many things in the future. I am positive that my brother realised that his life could move in one of two directions; what kind of man was he to become? He could easily slip into the role of Ireland's most arrogant, omnipotent teenager (he had, after all, managed to receive three vans from Henry Ford and a correspondence from Adolf Hitler); or he might become a man of grace and kindness. As much as I have criticised Devin for his outlandish schemes and flights of the fancy, I would be committing an injustice if I did not say that he was, at heart, kind and generous. He spoke what he felt and believed; often it was the bitter truth and because people hurt when they hear what they do not care to hear, they said all sorts of things about him. Any one of his critics who could have been there in the walled meadows that morning would have abdicated their hard feelings for my brother.

Devin walked slowly towards the driver with a friendly smile and an outstretched hand. He came close to the trembling man and said kindly,

"I hope you're not hurt bad."

"It's me knee a bit."

"Let me have a look."

Devin lifted the tattered trouser leg and examined the knee.

"I think you'll be fine."

"I'm sorry, sir, but me mind was on other things."

Devin nodded and put his arm around the man. And when Devin turned towards us, he was another man and I was so proud of him.

FIVE

The Dingle townsmen clustered around our fleet of vans, one slightly damaged now. Devin told them that the vehicles represented the first of many economic innovations which would come to the peninsula.

"Other fine lorries will advance your profit," he told them.

Of course there was immediate resistance. The first morning we went out to pick up milk from our suppliers a sweeping plan of boycott was launched against us. The farmers simply said there was no milk that day; the cows were resisting. It was not until the following week that we found out the reason. Part of the social life of the peninsula was the trip by donkey cart to the creameries. By cutting this off, the farmer was isolated from his fellowmen. It is a fact of Irish rural life that getting together or meeting at the crossroads, as they used to say, is the most looked forward to event of the week. Of course, Devin and I suspected this but we never thought it would go as far as refusing our pick-up of milk cans. Devin scheduled a meeting to be held in Uncle Shemas's old study. The whole company, consisting of Ronnie and myself, sat before Devin's desk. He did not for one minute bear the signs of defeat or setback, and he said in a bright hard voice,

"I was wrong. The people of this peninsula are not interested in change. So, despite our offer to use new vans for milk haulage at no cost to the farmer, they still would rather come to us on their donkey carts. Let that be; well and good. We shall move on to another plan. As we know, the railroad doesn't come to Dingle. Every consumer product is hauled in by van. I say we hit competition on the basis of lower prices, better haulage, new safe vans. Now the second stage is this: there is not one large refrigerated warehouse in Dingle. This means milk, fish and other perishable products must be hauled into town in small quantities since their life is short. I propose that we build a refrigerated warehouse on our property next to the quay. We will use that as the office of our hauling company and charge warehouse fees, naturally."

"And what would a warehouse cost?" I asked.

"Four thousand pounds," Devin answered.

I thought for a long time and saw, in a horrible image, our inheritance money going on the wind. Somehow, I must admit, I believed that Devin would connect and we would enjoy the profits of his schemes. So I nodded my head, "Yes", while a small tremble ran the length of my arms. I was committed to Devin. (God help me!)

In eleven weeks' time we had the warehouse up and the refrigeration plant going. Two local merchants were our first customers and soon the fishery was using our premises. We then found that cheese and milk began to smell like mackerel, so we partitioned off the warehouse into two units.

A new company was started—Ryan Brothers, Warehouse and Haulage. Large white letters told the town and strangers, too, that we were beginning to be a big business force in Dingle. Our vans worked day and night. Devin undercut the other haulage firms in Killarney so that our business flourished with milk and produce coming and going around the clock. Devin moved the executive offices from Uncle Shemas's study to a wing of the warehouse which he had furnished with a deep gold carpet, a large desk from Dublin and a secretary's office and reception room. No company on the whole peninsula had such comfortable or impressive quarters and when my teenage brother sat behind his seven foot desk, he was indeed an imposing sight. Shortly after our offices were finished, Devin went into Killarney to have a photo sitting. The large sepia print of Devin in a business suit which made him look a full twenty-five years was delivered in a gold frame to match the rug. Underneath, engraved on a bronze shield big enough for the words to be read across the whole room, was the title: DEVIN H. C. RYAN, OUR FOUNDER.

And this, as I remember, was the turning point. Our employees, now seven in number, began calling Devin not just "Mr. Ryan" but "Mr. Ryan, sir", and that was the name he wished to hear although he never demanded that anyone address him as such. But he was still Devin down at the "Bee" where my brother took his noontime meal and evening drink—a Martini, which he introduced to Dingle. (That alone, I admit, was something of a black legacy because it caused many problems in years to come, long after Devin was gone from the peninsula.)

One morning as we were making our Irish oatmeal and Limerick bacon for breakfast, a certain Mrs. O'Connor, "Widow" O'Connor, appeared at our door nicely dressed in a flowered hat with plastic cherries growing from the brim and a black coat with a fluffy fur collar of some sort. She was wrinkled, with long white hair which seemed to encroach on her forehead in an excessive manner. Her glasses were bent and old, but somehow she seemed much younger than her appearance allowed one to believe.

"Good morning, Mrs. O'Connor. I thought our appointment was at half-nine," Devin said.

"Good morning, sir. The coach, you see, was early. So I came straight on."

"This is my brother, Mr. Billy Ryan, Executive Vice-President of the corporation."

(Devin, I forgot to say, had incorporated our haulage and warehouse company in Delaware, in the United States. We had, according to necessary restrictions, established our main office in Wilmington—only a mailing address—and the branch office was in Dingle, County Kerry. This came about because of an article on the DuPont Company printed in *Fortune* magazine. Devin associated Wilmington with industrial success.)

The old woman bowed and said weakly, "I'm here about the employment."

"Yes. Would you come to our personal library with my brother and me."

Devin took his place around the desk and Mrs. O'Connor sat on the edge of the small Victorian chair never daring to look Devin in the face. This visit was another surprise and I could not understand why the woman had come to us.

"You see, Mrs. O'Connor, my brother and I are important Dingle executives, busy with meetings and business problems all the day long. You can imagine the tough competition and tax burdens two men like us are forced to face day in and day out."

"Oh yes," she said.

"Now, Mrs. O'Connor, we suffered a terrible loss just nine months ago to the day. Our Chairman of the Board, Shemas Ryan, passed on leaving the business responsibility to Devin and me. As tired executives, we frankly do not have time to repair our white business shirts or make meals or entertain our customers in a gracious manner."

"Oh, I do realise your problem," she said looking sorrowfully at Devin.

"Yes. Well, I am looking for the right person who can take over these important responsibilities."

"Are there children, Mr. Ryan?"

"There are no women in the house," Devin said quickly.

"I see. I've never worked for bachelor men before."

"What is the difference if a man eats the food or a woman eats the food, except that we eat more of it?"

"Oh, I have nothing against men."

"You have references?"

"I worked for a German family in Cork. Very nice refined people. And I learned the language and taught the

30

youngsters English. I cooked their meals, sewed and did the laundry. Mr. von Bilhuber said I was very good in the mending and repairing of his shirts. He was in the export trade."

"Did you make Martinis for your employer?"

"I . . . . ah . . . ."

"That is a drink, Mrs. O'Connor, which you will have to get on to."

"I'm sure that I could now," she answered.

"The pay is three pounds two a week. You'll have your room and keep. Your duties will be answering the telephone correctly, serving us breakfast in bed, fetching the groceries, doing the shirts and pressing our business suits, and generally keeping the house up to our standards—which are high."

Devin lowered his head to the desk and wiped his finger along a coat of dust.

"It is dirty at the moment because my brother and I have been too busy with business pressures to keep up our dusting."

"Oh, I understand, Mr. Ryan. Is this a Christian house?" she asked, seeing some rather colourful female studies upon the cover of several new magazines. (By this time, Devin was subscribing to twenty-nine magazines and seven newspapers, including the *Wall Street Journal*.)

"Of course, this is a Christian house. What else would it be?" he said swiftly.

"I'm sure it is," she said.

"When could you start, Mrs. O'Connor?"

"I would have to go back to Cork for my things."

"Ridiculous. We will send one of our new vans for your belongings and you could start this very day. I'll take your word that you can cook, but I must tell you that I have a fondness for French food, delicately prepared, naturally."

Devin had never tasted a French plate in his life, but we were receiving several gastronomical magazines which described gourmet meals and the recipes thereof.

"Is German cooking somewhat like French cooking?" asked Mrs. O'Connor.

"I suppose so," Devin said. "After all, Germany and France are close neighbours. It will be for you to learn the

French way of cooking. I am starting a wine cellar and you will be asked to learn the vintages. Can you do that?"

"I can read, Mr. Ryan. Are you saying that?"

"It helps, I suppose, to read the labels. But I want you, Mrs. O'Connor, to learn the arts of good living. We do not eat cabbage in this house or salt beef, and I want all the Irish oatmeal taken away and replaced by soft, light omelettes. In other words, this is a continental house. You see, my brother and I run an international company. We have offices in the United States. Have you heard of Wilmington?"

"I have not."

"It is a great industrial center, the hub of American business and enterprise—where the DuPonts live."

"I've heard of them," she answered.

"By the way, will you take a memo, Billy? Excuse me, Mrs. O'Connor."

Without thinking, I reached for a piece of paper and said, "Certainly."

"Please tell your staff to change the sign on our plant Number One to read: 'The Ryan Brothers International—Dingle, Ireland, and Wilmington, Delaware, the Republic of the United States.' I would like press releases sent out to the papers telling of our international operation. Let me read them before they are posted."

Devin then turned his head to Mrs. O'Connor who was sitting wide-mouthed.

"Do you understand the nature and importance of our business, Mrs. O'Connor?"

"Oh, indeed, I do."

"I think you have passed our employment qualifications. I'll show you to your quarters."

Devin rose and proceeded out of the room towards the upstairs of the house, and then said in a much less official voice, "It's nice to have you as a member of the firm. We'll all grow together."

I sat there in the morning light looking at the empty desk and the small chair where the Widow O'Connor had sat. It was then that I began to wonder and seriously speculate just where Devin Ryan and myself, for that matter, would end up.

SIX

Uncle Shemas's house underwent a violent change once Mrs. O'Connor was put in a position of authority. She was not the "lace curtain" type and, moved by Devin's imagination and dash, she ordered over nine hundred pounds worth of household improvements. These were delivered by our own vans from Dublin and included designer-patterned curtains, a giant bed for Devin who had moved into Uncle Shemas's larger corner room. When I came home for my noontime meal that day, the electric refrigerator and electric stove were being unloaded according to Devin's directions amidst the wild anticipation of Mrs. O'Connor.

"Devin," I said when all was secure and working, "don't you think you're spending too much for this sort of thing?"

"You see. . . . you see!" he sputtered, "you don't have faith in the future or what we can do. If you don't wish to eat the meals from our electric stove, you can always go down to the 'Bee' for kidney pie and Brussels sprouts."

Devin sat silently that evening at dinner. During dessert he finally said, "Whoever heard of a centrally heated home without electric cooking?"

"I just think, Devin, that your spending is wild. How many magazines are we subscribing to a month?"

"They're the fountain of my knowedge. I'm learning French from one, Italian from another. I am trying to obviate the provincialism of rural Ireland. Please listen to my decisions. They've been right so far."

And I must admit, even to this day, that Devin crashed into business on the right track and those who laughed at

33

his early farm reforms were now saying, "Yes, Mr. Ryan, sir" and "No, Mr. Ryan, sir". Devin was a force in Dingle and no one could dispute that point. I became accustomed to our new life more easily than I imagined. Mrs. O'Connor's French cooking was somewhat disappointing at the beginning and it came out, as I recall, half-Irish-half-French. The house was managed on a strict routine. Mrs. O'Connor was up by five in the morning because she attended six o'clock mass faithfully. We were awakened by eight. I took my morning meal in the kitchen. Devin, on the other hand, demanded to be served in bed. (He had seen a picture in one of the American magazines showing an old executive getting his orange juice and eggs in a breakfast tray rimmed by a fresh rose and the morning *New York Times*.) Devin copied the routine and the morning roses were trucked in from Killarney and *The New York Times* came by post.

Devin accepted his morning paper with eagerness even though it was about three weeks old. He read the stock market quotations and often commented on the world situation as if it were happening that very day. Another addition which came from Dublin was Devin's dictating machine, and I knew that a few more earth-shaking letters were about to originate from Dunratty House. By half-ten Devin, finished with his breakfast and dictation, would get into one of his eleven business suits, pressed and laid out by Mrs. O'Connor, and walk through the town to his warehouse office.

My own business day started at half-eight and when I spoke to Devin about his tardiness, he called me into his office and said, "I wanted to be rested and able to think clearly about new business expansion. I get all my finest ideas between the sheets, and I am not speaking of what you might be thinking. In fact, that's a part of my harried life that's seriously missing but I wouldn't take any of these Dingle girls as my wife. You probably don't know it, but a wife is an asset to a man's business career. However, I won't go into that now. I want to talk about some new ideas."

Devin strolled about and then gravely said to me, "I don't like the way the world is going."

"No one does."

"That letter we received from Mr. Hitler. . . . I somehow don't believe that man. So I wrote to Albert Schweitzer asking for his opinion."

"And what did Albert say?"

"I don't know. The letter was returned for insufficient postage, but three weeks ago I consulted the White House."

"In Washington?"

"Absolutely."

Devin handed me a copy of the correspondence to the President of the United States. A nervousness came on me as I read the preposterous words:

Mr. Franklin Delano Roosevelt
President of the United States
The White House
1600 Pennsylvania Avenue
Washington, D. C.
The United States of America

Dear President of the United States:

I am an Irish industrialist working with Henry Ford, Sr. on an expansion programme for the rural areas of County Kerry. Naturally, we wish to carry on our growth pattern, but I have been somewhat dismayed by the deterioration in the European situation. My late uncle and chairman of our firm (with offices in Wilmington, Delaware, and Dingle, County Kerry) said to us, "When doubt crosses your mind and you wish the right answers, go to the top." I have already gone to one top and I've enclosed copies of my correspondence with Adolf Hitler, the German leader.

As you can see from my correspondence to Mr. Hitler, I wished to know his intentions as I am sure all people would be interested in the same. His answer to me was satisfactory but somehow history tells us that all nations proceeding towards war are forever preaching peace. (Haven't you felt that this is the case, Mr. Roosevelt? I mean, in your own readings of history?)

The purpose of this letter is, naturally, to seek your

opinion. In other words, how do we stand? Are you pessimistic or optimistic about this fellow over in Germany?

I have noticed pictures of your little dog, Fala, in the press. On several occasions he looked rather cold running around in the snow in front of your house on Pennsylvania Avenue. I think small dogs should wear sweaters like most of us do so I have asked the head of my household staff, Mrs. O'Connor, to knit Fala an Irish wool sweater for winter wear. I hope he enjoys it.

My very best to all your family and say "hello" to Jim Farley for us.

Most sincerely,
Devin H. C. Ryan, Esq.

I scanned the words again and then backed slowly to the chair where I read the opening once more.

"Devin, how the hell can you write such a thing?"

"It was quite easy," he said mechanically.

"But this sentence about . . . . nations proceeding towards war are forever preaching peace . . . . where did you get that?"

"From Boswell."

"You steal sentences from other people?"

"Yes. I have several books on famous letters and I clip a few here and there. Oh, don't look at me like that, Billy! God knows, what original sentences are there left in the world? They found out that some of the things Caesar said were stolen from some Greek chap."

"Did you really think the President of the United States would answer this?"

A large smile seeped across Devin's face and I knew before he told me that there was, indeed, a response to the outrageous letter. I should say that the frightening part of Devin's letter writing was not his audacity, but rather the fact that everyone took him seriously. (Actually, his correspondences were well typed and presented; how did the President of the United States know whether Devin was an elder Irish intellectual or just a wild, ambitious boy?)

Devin then placed an envelope in my hands. In the upper left-hand corner it said with startling simplicity: THE WHITE HOUSE. I slowly slid the stiff letter out and opened it:

My dear Mr. Ryan:

How nice of you to send along a sweater for Fala. It fits well and I know it will keep him warm in the chilly months to come.

The Cabinet and myself were quite interested in your letter and the attached communication from the Reichsführer, Adolf Hitler. It sheds some new light on possible future relations between Engand and Germany. If you receive more letters from the Reichsführer, we hope you will share them with us.

No one can be totally optimistic over the European situation. Ours is a "wait-and-see" policy and we are keeping a close watch on all events. I would say that you should go ahead with your expansion program and if you have further ideas or information on the international situation, please do not hesitate to write or call me. We are particularly interested in the views of non-aligned small nations. People such as yourself who are not by implication or political alignment close to larger nations can sometimes stand apart and interpret a development with complete objectivity.

My wife, Eleanor, joins me in thanking you again for Fala's sweater.

I am most cordially,
Franklin Delano Roosevelt
President of the United States

"What can I say, Devin?"

"Isn't it interesting how things have developed? Eleven months ago they didn't even listen to me down at the 'Bee'. No one took Devin Ryan seriously and now, by God, the President of the United States wants my advice. Things can change, Billy; never forget that. And it all happened because of dear Uncle Shemas. God bless his soul!"

Devin then sunk down behind his desk and took out a

blood pressure machine which he attached to his arm and began inflating.

"Where did you get that?" I bellowed.

"Forget where I got it, my dear brother. Why don't you ask me *why* I got it. Well, I'll tell you straightaway."

Devin pointed to the needle on the gauge as he pumped.

"Where that needle goes decides many things for me, our company and who knows? . . . the whole future development of Ireland and the world."

"Devin, your imagination is going wild."

"Is this imagination?" he said, holding up the letter from President Roosevelt. "There is *no* imagination too wild or full blown."

"I don't know, Devin; I just don't know."

"I've taken the liberty of ordering three more vans from my friend, Henry Ford, Senior. I told him we were very pleased with his first three lorries and that we have decided to order additional equipment."

"Who is going to pay for these?"

"Long term loan, my dear brother. Everything is done on the long term loan basis these days. Why pay? Just or- and hope for the best. I believe there's going to be a war and if there is, we're going to be ready while we can still get vans. Hell, if there's a war, we'll be feeding England like we did last time but at higher prices. I've received permission from the Irish Ministry of Power and Transport to haul into Cohb and Dublin. Billy, our fortunes are about to be made!"

Devin, at that point, did not know how right he was.

The three new lorries were delivered to Galway City and we built an additional garage beside the warehouse. What amused me most during these months of 1939 was Devin's soaring imagination; it was like a crazy bee, believe me. I must say, I travelled along with him and his ideas because there seemed to be some response to everything he did. I suppose, too, that I merely kept to myself those things I wanted to say because I was deeply interested in just how far Devin Ryan could go. Lord, I never suspected just how far that was going to be.

SEVEN

During early June of that year, 1939, we motored up to Galway to pick up three new vans. And, I must say, that I felt proud as we took possession; it was our first step towards expansion and for a time I did not bother to examine the thinning line of credit. As soon as these vans were placed into operation, our entire company seemed to reach another dimension. We went from a rather loosely run hit-or-miss business propelled by Devin's whims into a more formalised organisation. During the early summer Devin himself was keen on supervising every detail of the corporation. Somewhere he had read about the "total look", the appearance of a company which should be saved at all costs even when the credit collectors were repossessing the investment.

And so we became appearance happy.

White uniforms were ordered for all the drivers; we placed advertisements in the papers announcing our extended haulage and warehouse facilities. Then Devin hired a certain Miss Tremble to keep things business-like. She was a tall, bony lady emerging on the far side of middle-age who had given courses in business practises at a County Cork nunnery. Miss Tremble possessed unusually sharp cheek bones and she had a way of casting her greyish eyes down upon you as she spoke. Indeed, it gave her a commanding sort of air. (To me, she was a chilly lady.) I never thought this practical woman and my erratic, colourful brother would get on and for a time I expected a terrible collision of words. But when Miss Tremble ordered the intercommunications system so that Devin could issue orders into a phone, he immediately changed his tone and said to me,

"You see, Billy, Miss Tremble, even though she looks like a sterilised hawk, really knows how to ease the burdens of a tired executive."

There was something else between those two—not a spoken communication or even an understanding—but rather a sense of playing the game of very big business. For instance, it did not take but a fortnight for Miss Tremble to realise all the fancies of my brother—his voracious appetite for writing letters and the pressure which he liked to believe he lived under.

For one thing, she managed to start a ledger outlining the birthdays and important events in the lives of great men. This was to feed Devin's ego like no other potion because it linked the intercommunication system with a message facility to the outside world. Often when dear Devin and I were arguing, and I must say, there were many discords in those days, Miss Tremble would interrupt—always when I was making my point—and Devin would let the loud buzzer go on and on as if he were suspended in thought. Finally, he would reach across his desk and say snappily,

"Yes, Miss Tremble?"

"Mr. Ryan, I forgot to tell you. George Bernard Shaw has a birthday tomorrow. Shall we wire?"

"Yes, of course, send Mr. Shaw my congratulations and tell him we are sending along a small jar of homegrown grape jelly. And, Miss Tremble, tell Mr. Shaw that I liked his criticism in the *Guardian* last month, or whenever it was."

Devin would press down the intercom key and turn his head towards me, wiping his brow and saying whispered words,

"I'll never last. I'll never last."

Then, as a diversionary manoeuvre, he would gobble a few pills given to him by Doctor Kilmartin and composed mostly of sugar (I later discovered). As he chewed the last of these, Devin would ease his hungry black eyes towards me and apply that hurt, helpless look to his face and say weakly,

". . . . you were saying, Billy?"

"Damn it! What's the use! What's the use!" I cried.

And he would only look towards me with more pain in his face, answering, "I'll never last."

There was no use arguing with Devin because he had too many planned distractions and it was hardly a secret that Miss Tremble was in on his stratagems.

But while these horrors took my sleep, we did show a fine profit during the late summer of '39 and that, I am quite certain, preserved the only peace left in my mind. Even though Devin was spending unheard of sums on caviar and imported vodka and buying clothes at such a rate that the tailor would motor all the way from Dublin for his fittings, he nevertheless made many correct business decisions. We hired a manager to run our creamery operation and made that another division of Ryan Brothers International. Added to this, we secured from the Ministry of Power and Transport an export licence so that, officially at least, we were in the business of international trade. Then Devin, in one particular stroke of good thought, purchased the small firm in Cork which had been exporting our milk fat products to England. This meant that the fat from our separators was shipped in our own vans to our own export outlet in Cork.

Now all this affluence shown by my brother had a certain uneasy effect upon the whole town and, especially, upon Father Dunn. Father always spoke out against the easy life, the life which was ruled and guided by corporeal pleasures. (In Ireland—a Jansenist, parochial community—guilt and a certain amount of humility, real and otherwise, happened to be the most accepted traits of the national life.) Devin had neither humility nor poverty and this, naturally, gave certain alarm to Father Dunn. He commenced this alarm some years before when he visited our home and found periodicals, some of which showed seductive females on the cover, resting all about, sometimes jammed in the whiskey closet. When Uncle Shemas passed, God bless his soul, Father Dunn, I am certain, believed that Devin and I committed moral suicide.

More and more worldly magazines arrived at our door;

41

Mrs. O'Connor was forever letting the town know that we were feasting on pheasant sandwiches and our caviar came the whole way from Russia.

Of course, Father Dunn believed that we were leading the whole town towards moral decay and often he would drop by the office, for just a word he used to say.

But these visits were warnings and nothing else. The poor priest became, just as I was, totally frustrated by the interruption conspiracy of Devin and Miss Tremble. One morning Father Dunn had dropped by after his mass and Devin was sermonising,

"You see, Father, in my opinion, God does not want indolence. You see, Christ himself wasn't a slacker. He worked around his father's carpentry shop. Now the trouble with too much spirituality, Father, is that people become over-involved with mystical things and they let this life go to seed."

"How is it you can talk like that, not having had one hour of theology or any godliness about you!" Father replied swiftly.

And then, as if planned like a stage play, the buzzer rung and Father Dunn jumped a bit.

"Yes, Miss Tremble?" Devin answered, shoving down the talk key.

"Mr. Ryan, you wanted to send the papal nuncio a donation for the new seminary in Spain. How much shall I draft from the bank?"

"Oh yes . . . . please draft 500 pounds and wire it today. Ask the papal nuncio to remember me in his mass."

"Thank you, Mr. Ryan."

"Thank you, Miss Tremble."

Then, of course, Devin grasped his sugar pills and Father stared at him, completely unhinged, not knowing how to continue.

"Why can't we discuss these things in the parochial house where we can relax over a sherry?" Father Dunn said pleadingly.

"There is no relaxation in this life, Father. I work day and night for one reason. I want the people of this small Irish community to have a better life. You look out into the green hills and you see beauty—little cottages, the smoke curling up from the peat fires, the lantern in the window, the soft chants of the rosary being said by a family kneeling on the damp, dirt floor. You know what you're looking at?"

"A nation of saints," Father Dunn said, his big eyes swelling with tears of love.

"You're looking at rural poverty! The same sort of depression which has ruined Ireland for hundreds of years. I want to change that; I want Ireland in the twentieth century and that is the nature of my deeds and the contents of my endless prayers to all the saints!"

"Are you a holy man, Devin? Is that your claim?"

"I don't know, but every day I have masses said for me all over Ireland. I had twenty masses said yesterday alone—a spiritual bombardment."

"That's my point, Devin. You believe you can buy your way into heaven."

"Can't you?" he said with a wink.

"No, Christ wasn't rich. His whole message spoke about the dignity of work and humility."

"No one works harder than I do, Father."

"I don't care what happens to your soul, but since you have taken over the economics of this town, the attendance at mass has fallen off and there is more drinking and betting than ever."

"The people have more money, that's all."

These dialogues between Father Dunn and Devin went on at least three times a week and I am sure that Father believed Devin to be a hedonist. The basis of the disharmonies between Father Dunn and Devin were, no doubt, rooted in my brother's quick and surprising rise to power in Dingle. Traditionally, the leader, spiritual and sometimes otherwise, in Irish towns was the local curate. He was the man with education and wisdom, and often in the absence of a local constable he was the quasi-sheriff. Father Dunn had enjoyed this position in Dingle for as long as I could remember. Often as we were growing up, Uncle Shemas would say, "Well, if you don't believe me, ask Father Dunn." The implication, of course, was that the priest knew everything. And Father, it must be said, took pleasure in this role. He was not only respected and the decider of morals, but he enjoyed a calm life within a fine greystone parochial house on the hill. As I have said, we *too* lived in a fine house; ours was more advanced since Uncle Shemas installed central heating and the priest warmed *his* place with peat.

When Uncle Shemas passed on, Devin immediately caught the imagination of everyone in Dingle, stealing some of the gleam and position enjoyed by Father Dunn. So there was rivalry, and quite logically the priest feared this new influence in what was originally a peaceful, moral-minded town not going anywhere or having plans for a dramatic future.

The conflict between Father and Devin never reached the acute, explosive stage during Devin's initial rise to power. This was due to another shrewd move on the part of our company president. Father Dunn (and I say this most respectfully) had a certain appreciation for the fine things in life. He liked flowers, and the parochial garden gave the priest endless hours of pleasure. But the joy of our youth was another hobby practised by Father Dunn; and that was his large gauge model steam railway which ran the length of the geraniums and curved easily behind the shrub bushes, emerging again on the far side of the parochial hydrangeas. Now it was never known how Father came upon the model steam trains; some said they were given to him as an ordainment present, but whatever, the little steam train was known to run its route in Father's garden before the time of our birth.

On Sundays, in the fine months, Uncle Shemas took us to see the trains. And it was a special treat or a reward just to stand there and watch the working steam engine burn bits of peat and make the far turn and race in front of the Statue of the Virgin Mary. I remember too, with clarity, how Father looked upon his model railway with a special sort of pride. And Devin, no doubt, recalled these visits to see the steam trains.

"How are your trains, Father?" Devin asked right in the middle of an unusually sharp argument with the priest.

"Oh . . . . the tracks are a bit rusted this year."

And then Devin went on telling the priest that having a hobby was important to preserve the moral fibre and, finally, my brother said with not the slightest hesitation in his voice,

"You know, Father, I like model trains, too. I've been very interested in railways."

And the two of them began a discussion on large and small trains which lasted well into the noontime meal hour. Devin was just as brilliant on trains as he had been on celery, and later that evening I knew why. Upon his bed was a stack of model railway magazines from five countries. I am sure that upon reading them once he picked up enough of the nomenclature to carry on a seemingly knowledgeable conversation with Father Dunn.

Devin's relationship with the priest was at a severe low point when my brother proposed to the priest that they should join hands on an expansion of Father's model railway. This, according to Devin, would bring them closer so they might resolve spiritual and worldly differences. Devin's contribution to their mutual hobby was the laying down of a second track in Father's garden. Also, he gave the priest a new steam engine imported from Austria at the cost of three hundred and forty pounds. When I received the invoice, I marched into Devin's office.

"Devin, we can't afford gifts of this sort!"

"These days corporations have to give presents to maintain the peace. Father Dunn even said a mass for my salvation this morning. Isn't that progress?"

"Devin, I'll say this for the last time, if you don't have respect for the pound, this company is heading towards financial disaster."

"You're always saying that, Billy, and yet our business has doubled in the last few weeks alone. I have great optimism for the future."

And, then, the buzzer sounded.

"Mr. Ryan, it's time for your pill. And Friday is Henry Ford's anniversary. Shall we wire?"

"Send him our congratulations and a jelly to Mrs. Ford."

I stormed out of the office slamming the door.

EIGHT

Around the first of June 1940, I sensed that something was about to happen. Devin became edgy; he stayed up until the early morning hours reading books and magazines on Britain. One morning he came into my small office saying his favorite words,

"I'll never last! I'll never last!"

"You look terrible, Devin. What's wrong?"

He slumped into the chair and said weakly, "The pressure. No one knows what I go through."

"Well, if it's pressure, you bring most of it on yourself."

"I'll never last. Well . . . . there's only one thing to do, Billy," he said pushing straight up to his feet. "We're taking our holiday in England. Now I don't want to hear all the reasons why we shouldn't go, the war, the rationing. I need a rest, a change of pace."

My natural reaction was a glum face, a fear of Devin running wild in London. At the same time, I had never been to England although I felt I knew the country a bit since Uncle Shemas spoke well of it. His sister, Mary Rose, now Reverend Mother Mary Rose, ran an orphanage for chronically ill children in the Lambeth district of London. Devin, I seem to recall, had made several donations to the Reverend Mother. He rationalised the holdiay, in part, by saying that we were going at the request of our aunt to review the needs of the orphanage. Actually, we had only seen Aunt Mary Rose one time and that was, I believe, when she met Uncle Shemas in Dublin sometime during 1934.

"It's all decided," Devin continued breathlessly. "Miss Tremble will run the business during the fortnight and

Aunt Mary Rose has booked us into a nice refined hotel near the orphanage."

On June 27, 1940 (how could I forget the date), we climbed into one of the vans hauling our cardboard suitcases bulging with Devin's wardrobe and Mrs. O'Connor's jellies prepared in case England ran out of food. We motored to Cobh and caught the nightboat for Wales.

Suddenly Devin lost his "international" polish and corporation manner and he became a boy again, filled with the excitement of the trip, the idea of being able to travel abroad and call the whole proceedings a business trip.

We found England quite different from Ireland. It was more civilised, I suppose, and less beautiful. During our train ride from Fishguard to London, we pressed our noses on the windows to see every detail of the countryside as it flashed by. We arrived at Paddington Station at half-three in the afternoon; it was steamily hot and a light rain fell. We were not out of the carriage more than a few minutes when we were swept up by the surging, short-tempered crowds rushing and pushing each other towards the street. There was a frightening noise to all this—the blare of horns, train whistles, shouts and the usual roar of London traffic on a wet afternoon. It was more people than we had seen and, certainly, no noise like this ever came upon us in the quiet of the Irish countryside.

Devin and I exchanged glances and I knew that our feelings were identical. Here we were—corporation executives, at least in our minds—coming out of the Irish countryside and being tossed like helpless little fish into the rude, live world of London at half-three on a Friday.

I do not know what we expected, but it was not this. We felt slightly nervous and Devin completely lost the brazen look which usually hung about his face. And he said to me, "I'll never last the day."

I believed that the same fate would fall upon both of us, some sort of punishment. I could see Devin's world collapsing; the make-believe identity he had created for himself was no longer effective. No one in London said, "Good Morning, Mr. Ryan, sir." What were we but two Irish lads, not so well presented, carrying cardboard suitcases and trying to make some sense out of perhaps the biggest, most confused city in the entire world.

We had been belched onto the puddle-filled pavement in front of Paddington Station and in a grand attempt to rid ourselves of the mob, we began running across the street. I cannot say what we were running from or running to, for that matter; it was merely a flight after some calm. We found a taxi stand some streets away and just as we were about to enter the cab, Devin's cardboard suitcase, saturated by the rain, came apart and his whole wardrobe was scattered into the filthy rain puddles of that London street. Soaking wet, he stopped, looked down and then brought his great eyes towards mine. He said not a word, but his whole stature as business executive and international man of letters was stripped bare. Oh, how he must have wished to be back in Dingle sitting in the "Bee" and having a quiet Martini.

The taxi ride was a skidding, hooter-blowing affair with the driver yelling, "Git over, will yuh, mate!" And, finally, after riding up one street and down another, we drew up to the kerb and the driver said, "That'll be eleven and six, mate."

We climbed out carrying our clothes which were now pressed into a round wet wad of stenchy wool. The building in front of us was the most depressing, ominous structure that I had ever seen. Being four stories, it was built during Victorian times, I guess, and the stones had long gone black with soot. Tall, vaulted hip roofs jabbed the sky and grotesque gargoyles looked down upon us.

"Is that St. Ann's Orphanage?" Devin asked the driver.

"That's it, mate. Eleven and six, please."

Devin reached into his pocket and handed the driver a collection of coins.

"What's this, mate?" the driver yelled back.

"The fare," Devin said, "eleven and six."

"Yuh can't use Irish coins around here, mate. Well, I can see you're a bogman just over, huh? Better get some proper shillings."

I suppose Devin's nerves were at a breaking point because he grabbed the driver by the collar and pulled the man's head out into the rain saying in a rough voice,

"I am a corporation president, you fool. You'll take

48

that money or I'll have you in the tank straightaway!"

A constable appeared out of the rain and he slowly released Devin's grip on the frightened driver.

"Arrest him, officer. He's one of those Irish troublemakers. Look what he forced upon me."

The driver was out of the cab by this time showing the officer the fistful of Irish shillings.

"Let me see your passport," the officer said to Devin looking at the ball of clothing in my brother's hands and the blood pressure gauge dangling down suspiciously like an article of stolen goods.

Instead of hastily presenting the passport, Devin pulled out a business card and showed it to the officer. He read the words: DEVIN H. C. RYAN, PRESIDENT RYAN BROTHERS INTERNATIONAL, INC. DINGLE, COUNTY KERRY, IRELAND; WILMINGTON, DELAWARE, U.S.A.

The officer peered into Devin's dripping face and he simply laughed.

"What are you trying to pull? Where did you steal this card?"

"I am an executive."

"Impersonating, are you? Trying to pass Irish money and I haven't seen your passport."

"We *are* executives," I said.

"Why don't you tell that tale to the sergeant."

"My aunt is the Reverend Mother in there," Devin said weakly while he pointed to the sinister structure before us.

"It's true; the Reverend Mother is our aunt. We came from Ireland to inspect the orphanage," I said.

"We'll just drop in and see."

The constable grabbed us hard by the arms, and, with the driver following, we were marched up the cracked steps of the old orphanage. The officer rang the bell, a mooing sort of tolling like the sound of death. One of the Sisters came to the door. She opened it slightly, thinking, of course, that the officer had two criminals under arrest. I felt exactly like a criminal and Devin's face had now gone ashen.

"These lads claim they know the Reverend Mother."

"Well, I don't know," the Sister answered.

"What's the name of the Mother Superior?" the officer barked at Devin.

"Reverend Mother Mary Rose. She's my aunt, my Uncle Shemas's sister."

"Well, yes, that is the name of our Reverend Mother," the nun said.

"Do you suppose she might identify these two. If she can't, we'll have to arrest them."

"And they owe me eleven and six," the driver added.

The nun invited us in and she disappeared down the long, dimly lit corridor which was speckled with falling plaster and in need of urgent repairs. We stood there in silence, dripping wet, and we heard far-off coughs of little children and footsteps over the wooden floors above. Then, a large nun with a very round face came floating out of the shadows and Devin said,

"Hello, Reverend Mother."

She stopped a minute not quite knowing how to react to the officer but once she recognized Devin, she rushed forward and embraced us together.

"You know them?" the officer asked.

"Of course. They are my nephews from Ireland."

The Reverend Mother settled our taxi bill and the disturbance was cleared up but Devin was abashed. He remained totally silent as Aunt Mary Rose took us around to the hotel, a small grey, oppressive looking building some three streets from the orphanage and called, quite correctly, The Crooked Hen. We were shown our room, a simple little place with a washstand and a dusty window which overlooked a faceless street.

Our entry into London was anything but spectacular and we felt more despondent when our aunt asked in a happy voice, "How do you like London so far?"

NINE

It rained through that night and into the early morning hours. Neither of us slept as I remember. The bed was uncomfortable; the hooters sounded through the night and the quarters possessed the pungent, annoying smell of coal smoke. (It was not the smell of quality coal smoke, the kind we had in the better districts of Dublin.) Without realising it and being quite good-hearted, Mother Mary Rose arranged a day of activities for us which only drove our depression deeper. She met us for breakfast that morning in the hotel and we sat and looked through the rain-beaded windows, drinking harsh coffee and trying to choke down the greasy eggs. This was followed by indigestion and a grand tour of the orphanage.

Mother Mary Rose was proud of what they had been able to accomplish with little or no funds. She showed us the newly decorated ward which was hard to distinguish from the old, undecorated ward; we saw the physiotherapy room; the pharmacy; and we met Doctor Hawkins, an ancient, retired medical man who was pressed into service to help the Sisters since they could hardly afford a full-time physician. Life at the orphanage brought great purpose and happiness to our aunt and the eleven Sisters under her.

But trying to smile into the hollow, hopeless eyes of the tiny orphans was almost more than we could bear. I suppose it was the doleful day, the dank building which looked as if it were about to collapse at any moment and the poverty under which the Sisters worked—all added together to give Devin and me the worst case of the shudders I can remember. We took our noontime meal in the nuns' refectory and after we had managed to hide that food in our napkins, Mother Mary Rose said cheerfully,

"I've arranged a nice coach tour for the afternoon and we are planning to see the wonderful sights of London."

At about two o'clock, we climbed on a crowded coach and sat ourselves in hard wicker seats as the tour started. The damp wool of our heavy suits began to bother the back of our legs and we scratched our way all around London in the steaming coach. Whatever the man on the loudspeaker said about Buckingham Palace or the Tower of London I do not recall, and neither of us cared a bit or gasped or wondered at the sights.

I think it was the comparison: here we sat, in rumpled, itching suits in a tour coach filthy with old Orange Crunch containers, watching the great chauffeured motor cars go by and distinguished looking men dashing about with their bowlers and brollies. Devin obviously wanted to be in that latter group.

And we started towards that goal at once.

Somewhere Devin had read that Claridge's was the place to stay while in London. We walked over there after the coach tour, holding the street map in our hands and looking, I suppose, like the peasantry in from a rebel country.

A high-hated officious doorman stopped us straightaway. I could tell how he sized us up. The wriggle to our suits, our bare heads and the map in our hands aroused his suspicions. And we failed to pass his scrutinising inspection.

"May I help you two?" he said sharply, holding his hand across the entrance to Claridge's.

"We would like a room for a couple of days."

The man immediately smiled and said in a rubbery voice, "And who recommended you?"

"We're executives."

"Of course you are. Get along now."

"I'm quite serious. We would care to see the manager," Devin answered.

"You just don't come off the street and register at Claridge's, young man. There're plenty of other places which cater to tourists. Be off with you now."

Hate and frustration came into Devin's eyes and he turned to me and said softly, "Billy, I'm going to walk a bit. I want to think. I have a lot to think about."

I understood.

He did not come back to the Crooked Hen until well after eleven that evening and when he entered the darkened room, he went straight on to bed without speaking. It was not until the following morning as we sat in the dining room trying to face the eggs again that I happened to look into his face. Of course, the sun was shining as brightly as it could through the sooty windows and, indeed, that might have accounted for some of the glow in my brother's face. There was something else I detected: that pussy cat grin which sat on his face always indicating that a scheme of grandeur was about to happen.

I was even more sure of it the following day because his grin was growing.

He left early in the morning and did not return until after half-eleven in the evening. He was not drinking; I was quite certain of that, but I could not imagine what was about to happen or why Devin had suddenly turned cheerful after our first shattering day in London.

The answer came one afternoon as I was having tea with Mother Mary Rose at the orphanage. One of the Sisters waddled in wide-eyed and there was a slight shortness to her breath, "Reverend Mother, there's an important gentleman to see you and Mr. Ryan. His driver asked for you both."

"What is his name, Sister?"

"He only said that you would know him, Reverend Mother."

The three of us bolted out of the parlour towards the front door. It was half open and, indeed, there stood a liveried driver with high, shined boots and a cap under his arms.

It was Ronnie Downs.

"Ronnie, what the devil are you doing in London?"

He winked and pointed towards the huge, shiny, black Rolls-Royce Silver Wraith sitting at the kerb like some sort of giant falcon taking its rest.

I knew the worst.

And in that moment *my* blood pressure went up. Devin had done it!

As we neared the motor car, I saw the words "Dunratty Castle" neatly printed just under the window on the rear door. Ronnie opened the door and lounging back with a frosty double Martini was Devin H. C. Ryan, Esq., in a bowler, black shoes, stiff collar and a dark blue double-breasted suit with a large silk handkerchief flowing out of his breast pocket. He smoked a heavy scented Sumatra cigar and said in a new tone, "Surprise, surprise."

This was the *new* Devin Ryan.

"What are you doing in that grand motor car, Devin?" the Reverend Mother asked.

"Needed something to uplift my spirits. Please step in; we'll tour a bit."

"Devin, you've rented this, haven't you?" I said, with a stammer in my voice.

"I bought it," he said as he drew in on the cigar.

"With what, Devin? Tell me!" I exploded. "You've gone crackers!"

"My dear boy, to be in London, one must look like London. Now get in and grow up."

"Devin, answer me. How did you get this car?"

"Long term loan. How did we come by the vans?"

"Is that true, Ronnie?" I asked.

"Indeed, it is. I think Mr. Ryan made an excellent choice."

"What did it cost, Devin?"

"Don't worry about that. It will increase our business."

"And what about that 'Dunratty Castle' on the door?"

"Oh, Billy, haven't you heard? A man's home is *always* his castle."

"I would like a ride, Devin," the Reverend Mother said, so proud that her nephew had somehow achieved a Rolls-Royce before his twenty-first birthday.

Traffic seemed to melt away in front of the Rolls; it is one of those definitive items in life which few will argue against or downgrade. Devin had arrived in London the only way he could and I should not have been surprised in the least; but, still, the motor car had to be paid for and I knew that was to be my job.

During the afternoon at tea time, we checked out of the Crooked Hen after placing Devin's six new suits in beautiful luggage he had purchased and then ruined, it seemed to me, with stickers saying: "Via Cunard First Class"; "Via P.&O. Orient, First Class". We drove up New Bond Street in silence; when we turned down Brook Street, I knew.

The very same doorman at Claridge's rushed over to help us, stopping momentarily to read the words: "Dunratty Castle". Ronnie Downs leaned out of his window in what was, obviously, a well-rehearsed opening line,

"Squire Devin Ryan and his brother have arrived to register."

"Yes sir!" the doorman rang out as he hustled the bags from the front.

Devin eased himself from the motor car taking in a huge gulp of air. He looked straight towards the doorman but the latter did not show the slightest sign of recognition. I strolled in behind my swaggering brother who stood in the centre of the main reception area looking about with his chin up and leaning on the tightly rolled brolly. The outside doorman gave the bags to the inside porter who quickly went to the desk. I noticed from the very corner of my eyes that there was a scurry about the reception area. Naturally, they were looking for the Ryan reservation. An assistant manager, pretending to carry on some business by the front entrance, walked past us and looked at the Rolls, just close enough so that he could read the small letters on the side of the door. He whispered something to the porter and returned to the reception desk. Two other men joined him and there was a conference and great shakings of heads and hidden looks in Devin's direction. I simply leaned from one leg to another with my hands dug awkwardly into my pockets highly embarrassed at a scene which Devin was enjoying to the fullest.

A swallow-coated assistant manager then approached Devin.

"Mr. Ryan, welcome to Claridge's. Won't you step into my office?"

I was introduced off-handedly and we followed the man

55

into a plush little office with a writing table and several velvet-covered chairs.

"Mr. Ryan, we have done something which almost never happens at Claridge's."

"And what is that?"

"We have misplaced your reservation."

"I wired on from my castle in Ireland. Oh, I should say that my social secretary wired at the request of Mr. Henry Ford, Senior."

At that point, Devin took out one of the letters from Henry Ford and held it in a certain way so the assistant manager could read the salutation just below the imposing Ford trademark and the smaller letters saying: Office of Henry Ford, Sr.

"I don't see it here. Could Mr. Ford have recommended me to some other hotel? The Ritz perhaps . . . . the mistake might be on our part," Devin said.

"Oh no," the assistant manager burst out politely, "Mr. Ford always stays with us. I am sure he would recommend Claridge's. I'll just put on the card . . . . recommended by Henry Ford, Sr. And, obviously, you'll desire the sitting room suite."

"Very good," Devin said mechanically.

It was the most magnificient two rooms in the world filled with rich antiques and a picture of Himself—King George VI. Those days following our entry into Claridge's were the most pleasant of my whole life. The raids were coming but in those weeks before the hell, London took on a carnival air; we spent seven hundred pounds and rode and rode in the Rolls and ate the best meals in town.

I liked being the brother of Devin Ryan.

TEN

The first air attack came on a Tuesday evening. I do not remember exactly the date; but Devin and I were planning to leave for Ireland the following day and, actually, we had stopped at St. Ann's to bid goodbye to the Reverend Mother. She served us tea and cakes and we were talking about the war in Europe when Ronnie Downs dashed into the blacked-out room.

"They say it's no test, Mr. Ryan. I've heard the planes overhead."

"Oh my God, we must get the children to the cellar!" our aunt said, crossing herself.

Ronnie was right.

A bomb exploded somewhere and it sounded like a far-off thud. Devin raced down the hall of the orphanage and the sounds became louder. On the street, a scattering cf helmeted wardens ran about directing people to the shelters. I must admit that it looked rather beautiful: the searchlights criss-crossing the sky, the tracer bullets reaching up like fireworks and explosions of the shells. We stood on the porch of St. Ann's and a bomb burst somewhere down the street. Bits of brick and other debris rained down upon us and, finally, Devin stood up and screamed,

"That man promised me there wasn't going to be a war!"

"I never did think he was telling the truth," I answered.

"The Rolls! My God, the Rolls!" Devin screamed as he leaped off the steps towards the curb. We were stopped by a warden.

"Better get inside, young man."

"That's my motor car. I just bought it!" Devin blasted out.

"Fine, but where do you plan to take it?"

"To a shelter! Anyplace! If I leave it here . . . . it'll be ruined."

The warden wouldn't let us drive the motor car away and he directed us back ino the orphanage; we walked through the old halls toward the red light which marked the stairs to the cellar. Another bomb landed nearer this time. Glass was broken around us and plaster drifted down from the weathered ceiling.

Another explosion followed which rocked the whole structure and it was easy to understand that St. Ann's Orphanage would never survive the war even if it were not directly hit.

When the all-clear sounded, Devin leaped from the cellar shelter to the street. Under the light of his torch, we saw to our horror that the Rolls was badly damaged. Shrapnel had peeled back part of the side and one could no longer read the letters "Dunratty Castle" on the door. Our windows were shattered and there were eleven bullet holes from a burst of a Spitfire's guns across the bonnet and two across the back. Devin put his hands over his head, leaned against the side and began to cry.

"He'll pay for this, the lying bastard!"

"Devin, I know it's a terrible thing . . . . your motor car being hit in the first air attack. But we can get it fixed, I'm certain," I said.

Somehow the vehicle did run and we limped back through the darkened bomb-pocked streets of London to Claridge's.

"My word, I hope you're not hurt, Mr. Ryan?" the doorman said as he inspected the Rolls.

"I'm quite all right. But he'll pay for this."

A small crowd gathered about the motor car looking at the damage. (To see a shot-up Rolls in the first air attack meant, I suppose, that nothing could be expected to remain sacred in the conflict to come.)

The next morning we drove the battered Rolls to the dealer in Berkeley Square. They slowly opened the twin glass doors for us and stood with bowed heads as Ronnie drove the hurt vehicle inside. It was as if a great bomber, injured in some important raid, were being pushed into the hangar for repairs and all the mechanics rushed over to see the damage and slowly shake their heads.

"Dreadful!"

"Incredible!"

"Please accept our sympathies, Mr. Ryan."

"I'd like an estimate. I'm sending it straight on to Berlin." My brother was quite serious because that afternoon with a copy of the repair estimate for three hundred and nineteen guineas, he composed the following correspondence on the stationery of Claridge's:

Claridge's
Brook Street, W-I.

Adolf Hitler
Reichsführer
Reich Chancellery
Berlin, Germany

Dear Mr. Hitler:

Last night, at approximately ten minutes past ten in the evening, your planes attacked London and one of your bombs fell near my aunt's orphanage in the Lambeth district. My new Rolls-Royce Wraith, recently purchased, was damaged and the repairs to this car will cost three hundred and nineteen guineas. I feel that since you spoke of peace in your last letter to me saying that the danger did not lie with Germany but with England, your raid on this capital, unprovoked as it was, showed that your intentions were warlike all along. I am a neutral and so is my new motor car and frankly, Mr. Hitler, I do not see why I should have to pay for something in which I have no involvement.

Furthermore, you assured me of your peaceful aims and, based upon your statements, I went ahead and ordered three new vans from my friend, Henry Ford. This war which you started will set us back considerably and, frankly, I am quite fearful of all the little sick orphans that my aunt and her nuns are trying to look after. The orphanage in the Lambeth district is an old building and it will not stand too many attacks.

Since you have inconvenienced me considerably and threatened the relations between our two countries, I shall have to ask you not to drop any more bombs on that part of London. I toured the area this morning in what is left of my motor car, and the whole place is not worth bombing. There was not one single target worth your efforts.

I have enclosed an estimate for repairs to my car and I know you will take care of this through the German Minister in Dublin in the shortest possible time. I hope that you will see the folly of this war you are starting and come to your senses and bring the hostilities to an immediate halt.

> Sincerely,
> Devin H. C. Ryan, Esq.

P.S. My friend, President Roosevelt, did not believe one word of your letter to me. I should have believed him rather than you.

"Are you serious, Devin?"

"You're damned right I'm serious."

As we were posting the preposterous letter to Mr. Hitler, the sirens wailed again. But we were prepared this time—the Rolls was deep in a garage and we elected to sit out the fire raid in the grill of Claridge's which had somehow been designated as a shelter. The atmosphere was quite pleasant and we met many interesting people over drinks while the bombs came down.

After the raid, Devin and I got a call through to our aunt who said that the orphanage had come through another raid with the children and Sisters acting as bravely as before.

The following morning we motored over to Lambeth. (On the trip, traffic officers seemed to let us go straight on and we came to realise that a war-injured Rolls was a certain mark of distinction.)

The facade of the old orphanage did not come through the attack nearly as well as Mother Mary Rose had indicated over the phone. Large percussive cracks ran the length of the second and third floors; windows were knocked out and now covered with cardboard and several gargoyles had already crashed to the street from their high perch. Inside, the situation was even worse. Fallen plaster was everywhere; water dripped from wrenched pipes; children were crying and the gas oven was out of order so that no hot meals could be taken to the wards. The Reverend Mother tried to speak resolutely saying that they would get by with God's grace, and Devin looking tearfully at the condition of one upstairs ward put his arm around the nun and made one of the great declarations of his life.

"Aunt Mary Rose, I believe in God's grace and the power of prayer. But let's face some facts. This building is not going to stand up to the attacks. It will collapse and all the orphans will be killed."

"I have a feeling you are right, Devin."

"Now, Reverend Mother, while I was drinking my Martini during the raid last night, a slight vision came upon me. I have decided what to do. I am moving the entire orphanage to the beautiful country around Dingle. You'll be safe from the war and the children can take the fresh sea air."

"How could we do that, Devin?"

"I plan to build an orphanage in Dingle. In the meantime, you can occupy some areas of our warehouse as temporary quarters."

"Who will pay for this?" the nun asked.

"I will . . . . our company, The Ryan Brothers International."

I realised the generosity and, perhaps, necessity of Devin's offer, but to move fifty-six orphans plus the nuns and equipment to Dingle represented a task which I knew we could not undertake. I told Devin this on the return trip to Claridge's.

"Billy, life has to be made of generous acts."

"How can we pay for this?"

"I'll never last if you bother me with details like that. The most important point is to get those children out of here. I might ask Henry Ford for a loan . . . . I don't know."

The doorman at Claridge's came to us immediately as we stepped out in front of the hotel and there was a look of seriousness upon his face.

"Mr. Ryan, those two gentlemen there are from the Foreign Office. They wish to see you on a matter of urgency."

"I'll receive them in my room, thank you."

The two men, tall, moustached and equipped with brollies and raincoats, inspected the Rolls noting with interest the bullet holes in the bonnet. They followed us into the hotel and appeared with us at the door to our suite.

"May we have a word with you, Mr. Ryan?"

Devin invited them in and we settled in the sitting room. One of them produced the letter Devin had addressed to Mr. Hitler.

"What do you mean . . . . tampering with His Majesty's Mail?" Devin shouted at the top of his lungs. "That was a private letter to Hitler."

"Well, Mr. Ryan, owing to the present situation, the war I mean, our superiors have instructed us to open all outgoing post to Germany. You might not have realised it, sir, but there is no longer a post service between the two countries."

"You might have returned the letter to me without opening it."

"We're following orders, Mr. Ryan. Might we inquire about your relationship with Hitler and President Roosevelt?"

"It's very simple. I've written to them before asking for their opinions on the state of the world situation. My brother and I are executives in Ireland and we only want peace so we may reach our growth targets."

"And you wrote to Hitler asking him his intentions. Is this true?"

"Of course."

"And he answered?"

"Indeed, he did. He said that the world should fear England, *not* Germany, and that Mr. Chamberlain would straighten everything out at the Munich conference."

"Hitler was quite wrong, wasn't he?"

"Right or wrong, I do wish to re-post my letter," Devin said.

"What is the nature of your business, Mr. Ryan?"

"We're in haulage and warehousing."

"I see. And what is the nature of your trip to Britain?"

"We simply wished to visit my aunt who is the Mother Superior of an orphanage in Lambeth."

"I gathered that from your letter to Hitler."

"And how, may we ask, did your motor car suffer bullet holes?" the second officer asked.

"It was in the street near the orphanage when the German planes attacked."

"And you expect Hitler to pay for the damages?" the man said wide-eyed.

"Wouldn't *you* send him a bill if your new car were damaged?"

They looked at each other and then at Devin and one of them said hesitantly, "I don't know."

"Thank you very much, Mr. Ryan," the other man said. "Now we would like to ask your brother a few questions in private. Perhaps we should retire to another room."

"I'll never last. I'll never last. Never!" Devin left the room and the two officers looked after him for quite a while. They finally turned their dull faces towards me and began asking a set of leading questions, but I knew at once what they were on to.

"Mr. Ryan, your brother seems so young to operate a Rolls and be a company president."

"He's just twenty, but very brilliant."

"We're sure he is," they said. "How long has your brother been corresponding with world leaders?"

"Oh, I would say, about a year now. Our Uncle Shemas who died about eighteen months ago told Devin to go to the top. You see, Devin wasn't having much luck writing to the vegetable editor . . ."

"What was that? The vegetable editor?"

"The editor of an American agricultural magazine."

"I see. Your brother writes to magazines?"

"All the time."

"Do you think it is unusual that your brother writes letters like this?"

"Well, I used to believe it rather odd and naive, but everyone answered Devin so who was I to say it was odd?"

"Do *you* feel that Hitler will answer this?"

"I don't know. He answered the last one."

"Mr. Ryan, has your brother ever been ill?"

"He had the usual childhood diseases."

"Has he ever been upset or done irrational, hasty things?"

"He bought the Rolls-Royce."

"Did you ever consult a doctor for nervous problems?"

"Devin thinks he has high blood pressure."

"Does he?"

"I don't think so."

"Has there been a history of mental illness in your family?"

"We were all quite sane."

"Your brother has never been committed to the asylum?"

"Now listen . . . . he's mad, but not mad-mad. Do you know what I mean?"

"I think we do. Well, Mr. Ryan, here is your brother's letter to Mr. Hitler. We would appreciate it if he did not post this from England. Naturally, a report of this matter will be forwarded to the Minister of Foreign Affairs in Dublin. I hope you will understand."

They stood, smiled and left.

Perhaps Devin was mad, but his madness was built of love and joy and it was delightful to my mind.

ELEVEN

Devin, in his sweeping goodwill gesture to remove our aunt's entire orphanage from Lambeth, London, to Dingle, Kerry, failed to realise the almost unsurmountable logistical problems. Obviously, England was not prepared for war: the phones broke down, medicines and some foods were difficult to fetch in those first weeks of the blitz and, generally, there was confusion all about. It was the *worst* time to transport sick orphans. I reminded Devin of this but he simply said that big business thinking and organisation could accomplish anything. And his fertile mind was already moving ahead.

We were walking in the rear of the orphanage across a courtyard which was, I suppose, a play area of some sort and we discovered an old double-decker London bus pushed against a stone wall. There was rust all about the vehicle now; some of the windows were out and the four wheel hubs were resting flat on the dried up tyres. We stepped aboard and climbed the curving stairs and I could tell Devin was thinking, imagining, because there was that look upon his face. He ran out of the bus and returned shortly from the orphanage with a measuring stick and he took the dimensions across the breadth of the bus on both levels.

"It'll work, Billy. We can arrange twenty-seven little beds across the coach and the other children, those who can walk, will go in our vans."

"You don't expect this thing to run, do you?" I asked.

"I'll take care of that. Now we must get our vans over here and start packing."

Devin explained his plan to the Reverend Mother and she told him straight off that the old coach never ran a day in its life.

"Some benefactor purchased it when they were about to junk it. It was towed here and that was that," she said.

"But I'll get it running. Ronnie Downs and I will see to it, Mother Mary."

The poor nun who was confused and speechless by this time merely said that everything was in the hands of God and Devin Ryan.

So, we began the job of moving the orphanage. Petrol rationing had gone into effect both in Ireland and England; finally, when Devin was able to get through to Miss Tremble who was so upset by the hostilities that she could hardly speak, they devised a plan whereby they would load the six vans with food products, apply for emergency petrol and bring the vans over via nightboat

65

from Cobh. This part of the plan sounded quite logical and obvious; less obvious was Devin's ideas for turning the 1929 double-decker bus into an ambulance which could haul the children all the way to Dingle. I do not believe that Mother Mary in her wildest dreams thought she would ever leave the old building. The poor thing was in a panic. The water pressure in her hoary building failed and part of the rear stairs collapsed sending heaps of rotten wood into the old linen room. I think the nuns were in such a state of shock that they listened to Devin as if he were a messenger from the Lord. The only other two men around the place were Jilly, a drunken janitor who slept most of the time on the far side of the coalbin, and old Doctor Hawkins who did not quite understand the meaning of the bombs. (During two of the raids, he meandered around saying, "Who is bombing us?") Devin assumed authority just as he did in Dingle, but I for one had some doubts.

It was the following day, after a nightmare raid which shook the orphanage closer than ever to collapse, that Devin and I visited the bus garage in Bayswater. As we drove in the entrance every mechanic in the place left his job to inspect the wounded Rolls. Ronnie leaned out to one of the foreman saying, "My good man, Mr. Devin Ryan would like to see the head mechanic straight away."

Soon a huge gentleman in a long white coat came towards the Rolls. Devin climbed out and introduced himself.

"You had quite a time with your Rolls, sir."

"Yes, we took a couple on the chin."

"Hope you weren't in there when that happened."

"Luckily, we weren't. Now, sir, I have a problem."

"I'm afraid the only thing we repair here are the public busses."

"Oh yes, I quite understand. That's exactly what we have—one old bus."

Devin and I were taken into the office of the head mechanic. We finally identified the type of vehicle we had on our hands. The man told us that it would be impossible to repair the bus; the parts were no longer stocked and the vehicle was out of date. But Devin had it in his mind to put that bus into running shape, and I'm sure his stubbornness had to do with Mother Mary's faith that he would save the lot of them.

"Who is the chairman of this omnibus company?" Devin asked, obviously preparing once again to go to the top.

It was explained to us that the company was part of the Ministry of Transport but it did have a chairman, one Sir Robert Eldon, O.B.E. We got through to Sir Robert that afternoon. Devin told the man he was chairman of St. Ann's Orphanage, Lambeth, and that he must see Sir Robert straight away on a matter of life and death. The man, who I imagine must have been working day and night on the war crisis, agreed to meet us at his country estate in Aylesbury outside London.

We motored up there crawling through the small country towns behind lines of war shipments which were clogging the thin English roads. I was not noticing the countryside that afternoon, but rather the people who stared after our bullet-riddled Rolls.

Sir Robert was in his vegetable patch to the side of the Tudor house as we drove up the crushed bluestone driveway at Aylesbury. He was a jolly fat man with a red face and teeth which popped out of his broad lips at an alarming angle. He stood straight upon hearing our motor and, in that second, I realised that we had won. Sir Robert had a Rolls, too.

He looked towards our damaged vehicle, then towards his own Rolls, hardly believing his eyes and in one giant leap, he came through his vegetables towards us. Devin climbed out and he leaned against the car as if slightly hurt.

"My God, man, did that just happen?"

"The other night. You are Sir Robert?"

"Yes. Oh, this is incredible," the fat man said, running his hands over the bullet holes. "Oh, what are we ever to do? Were you hurt?"

"Just weakened a bit. You know how it is—working day and night on my favorite charity."

"And you're so young. I do suppose your father sits."

"He did until he passed on."

"Oh my. Well, come in for tea. I want to help you any way I can. What an outrage, this war."

"I'm afraid things will never be the same again."

"No, it's beyond belief."

"Lights are going out all over the world," Devin said, as we walked along after Sir Robert towards the Cotswold Tudor house rimmed with flowers. I took Devin aside, whispering,

"Devin, do you have to use those expressions like 'the lights going out'? Where did you read that?"

"In the *Times* this morning," Devin answered without blinking.

"Let's just get to the point and not take too much of this man's time."

Of course, my advice did not fit into Devin's plans. Sir Robert brought us to a beautiful Linenfold paneled study and we sank down in great leather chairs. (From my place, I could see beyond the window as Ronnie Downs was proudly showing the whole household staff our riddled Rolls, I am certain that a story went along with each rip in the metal.) And a bombastic tale was starting within the study as Sir Robert and Devin began on double Martinis.

"My friend, F.D.R., told me long ago that this Hitler was up to no good," Devin said.

"I knew it all along."

"I've decided to fight on the homefront, Sir Robert. My brother and I run an extensive Irish haulage operation and we're trying to feed England as best we can; but I tell you—my blood pressure is up. I'll never last."

"My blood pressure has started up, also. I've just come from the doctor. That's why I am home this afternoon instead of down at that madhouse, the Ministry of Transport."

"Sir Robert, I want you to help me take fifty-four sick little British orphans to Ireland, away from this noise and holocaust. They won't survive at St. Ann's in that frightful old hell hole. It'll fall upon the children any minute if we don't fetch them out of there."

"Brilliant thought, Mr. Ryan. What can I do?"

"Frankly, we must rebuild a 1928 Model 18-B double-decker omnibus."

"My God, I haven't seen one of those around in years."

"The orphanage had one donated years ago. Of course, it doesn't run and your head mechanic told me we could never put the thing in order."

"Oh rubbish! Anything can be done. I am a man who can accomplish the most futile, hopeless task."

And that remark so echoed Devin Ryan's philosophy that I thought it must have been authored solely for my brother's ears.

The stories and philosophising went on until the early hours and we sat drinking Martinis and listening to the bombs come down upon far-off London. I said a prayer that Mother Mary and her orphanage would survive another night and that Sir Robert who seemed to be a fine man would see his way to helping us.

And indeed he did.

We came to the orphanage early in the morning and Mother Mary was brighter this day saying that no bombs had landed nearby and that the water heater and stove were somehow back in operation. Shortly after, three mechanics arrived from the Ministry of Transport. They asked to see the old bus and began making a systematic study of the frame and motor, noting, as best they could each part which might be needed. And that afternoon our six vans arrived from London.

This was the start of Devin's most monumental task of organisation and accomplishment. My brother had such a way about him that it was a sheer delight to see him those days. I only wished Father Dunn could have been present to watch Devin—how he issued orders; reassured the nuns who reassured the children; how he began a system of inventorying the entire pharmacy, the food stores on hand, the enroute plans for cooking and administering medicine to the children; and his firmness with old Doctor Hawkins which, indeed, straightened the befuddled man out. I never remember seeing Devin quite so happy; his life had suddenly been filled with a great purpose. And I think in those days Devin grew again as he had when he held back from hitting the whiskey driver who smashed our first van.

The orphanage turned into a busy place. The local priest came by to help and lend his moral support. Everyone seemed to centre his interest on Devin's main purpose—that of reconstructing the bus. Sir Robert pitched into this fun, too, about half-four each day after his work at the Ministry. (I was amazed how well the project went when the chairman himself was giving the orders.) The entire interior of the bus was stripped and floor sockets put in to hold the legs of the tiny beds. Then new glass was fashioned onto the windows; fresh tyres and rims were brought from somewhere and, virtually, a new engine with rebored cylinders, a new crank shaft made by a machine shop and all new rings and sparks, were installed in the housing. Even the varnished wood of the window trim was taken down and rebuilt. Altogether, I counted over sixteen craftsmen and mechanics labouring on the bus.

It was all to be attributed to a bullet-torn Rolls and the magic of Devin Ryan.

Finally, after four days, the paint crew arrived with their sprayers and Devin had them mix the exact green colour as the sides of our vans. The bus was sprayed nine times with enamel. It was such a beautiful job of restoration that the word spread about London and antique car enthusiasts came from all about to see the old bus which was in better shape than ever. The words, "St. Ann's Orphanage, Dingle, County Kerry, Ireland, formerly of Lambeth, London", were printed upon the sides in gold leaf, and then in smaller letters. "Reverend Mother Mary Rose, Superior".

Our drivers with the help of friends and neighbours loaded the vans with all the equipment from the orphanage; and in the back courtyard we assembled for the christening of the old bus conducted by the local curate, one Father Hansom. He said a few words about the generosity of my brother, Sir Robert and the Ministry of Transport; the latter I am sure had no knowledge of the repair project. In fact, Sir Robert gulped a bit when the priest mentioned the Ministry of Transport.

The children were carried out of the hospital in their beds and placed into the double-decker bus through enlarged doors. The whole loading operation took but a few hours; and by half-seven after a meal of hot soup and sandwiches, the motor convoy pulled out headed towards Wales. Mother Mary Rose with her few possessions rode in the Rolls with Devin and me while the other nuns accompanied the children in the bus which turned out to be a magnificent ambulance. (And quite fun for the children, I'm sure.) I remember so well that several of the nuns were crying as we left. They knew they would never see the orphanage again. (Three weeks later, we learned the place took a direct hit. The old bricks tumbled down and it was left as a pile of rubble.)

The old bus rattled and clattered despite its new condition; and as it was designed for the level streets of the city, the hills of Wales presented some problems. On the steeper inclines it had to be towed by one of our vans in order to make the grade.

Slowly and almost on schedule, Devin's convoy reached Fishguard. By this time, the nuns were beside themselves with joy and Devin was completely worn out as the days of work and excitement began to take their toll. (I noticed him on the boat taking his blood pressure while holding to the side of one of the lifeboats.) On the cross channel trip, which was calm, the nuns prayed that a U-boat would not attack and I, too, joined them thinking that this would be the final irony to Devin's greatest deed.

But God gave us His grace and we landed at Cobh the following morning and started down through County Cork to Kerry. About half-three in the afternoon we arrived in Dingle. Miss Tremble and most of the town were there to greet us. The women made hot soup and they turned out with what little they had to help the nuns and children. Already the efficient Miss Tremble had made two wards of our warehouse and our offices were to be turned into nuns' quarters until some more permanent quarters could be found.

Devin was silent and blank when we reached Dingle and he was not even there when Father Dunn came by to bless the nuns and the children. Devin was off to the "Bee" to have a Martini alone and Father Dunn said to me,

"Billy, perhaps I was wrong about Devin. God makes his good workers in all sorts of ways."

And I had to agree.

TWELVE

It was evident that the orphanage had to be removed from the warehouse straightaway if we were to stay in business, and Devin came up with the answer. Four years before, Uncle Shemas had decided to run an experimental milk producing farm on eight acres adjacent to our Dingle creamery. He had the idea of breeding a Kerry cow with another strain from northern Scotland in hopes of increasing the milk production. With some government help, as I remember, a huge modern barn was built near our creamery. It was a large one-storey structure of grey stone and had a cement floor. (The Ministry of Agriculture had halted the project and the barn lay idle.) The building full of windows and large doors was originally considered by us to become the refrigerated warehouse, but the multiple openings obviated that plan. However, we did intend to use the place for an auxiliary warehouse if that ever became necessary.

During the next few weeks Father Dunn joined Devin, and they pulled the whole town behind them to finish off the barn and prepare it for the children. We sent vans out all over Ireland with what little petrol we could get fetching fixtures and supplies for the new building, and most of the work was completed by local people. It took but three weeks to finish off the structure and install central heating. We partitioned the inside of the barn and each of the nuns had a small room; and we further divided the area into a refectory, treatment room, pharmacy, linen and supply room, besides a play area and a physiotherapy room. During these days Dr. Kilmartin and Dr. Hawkins worked side by side and I can say the whole town took on a unified task. For one thing, it brought all of them together in work, and old griefs and discords were forgotten. Dingle became a proud place.

It was four or five weeks later, after the orphans and nuns had moved into the new building, that the crisis struck. And it was the financial plague, something which I had feared the whole time through. First of all, we had never bothered to investigate the nuns' financial position, and when I happened to ask Sister Mary who sponsored her orphanage, she said simply, "The church". I assumed, and I believe Devin thought the same, that the church donations would come on to her in Ireland as they had in London.

But we were wrong.

We learned after several appeals to the Archbishop of London that he could no longer release funds for the orphanage, some four hundred pounds a week, because the charity was removed from his jurisdiction. The prelate said in a correspondence to us that he appreciated our good works in taking the children from London and that he would write a letter of recommendation to the Bishop of Cork. That latter diocese did manage to come through with some sixty pounds a week, which, I am sure, was a large amount for them; but this left quite a financial gap still. Of course, we were able to supply about one-half of the food for the orphanage, through donations by the local farmers, but the medicines and special equipment could not be offered locally. And then we were faced with the payments to the banks for our vans; also, we had to commence the monthly installments on the bullet-riddled Rolls.

The crisis was further complicated by the near collapse of our own business. Since petrol was rationed, our vans could not reach the export facilities in Cork. That meant it was impossible to take part in the wave of food shipments heading for England. Our competitors, those in the eastern part of Ireland, took up the trade.

It was a time of special tragedy for my brother. Everything came down upon him at once. His blood pressure went up legitimately. We no longer could feast on caviar and our meals became more rudimentary and basic as the weeks went on. But Mrs. O'Connor stood by with a reduction in salary and Miss Tremble stayed on also. Devin felt that it was his responsibility to care for the orphanage and by the early part of November, my brother had become more and more depressed.

I recall with a special kind of clarity the night the fateful adventure began. Devin, more downhearted than ever, retired to the "Bee". Mrs. O'Connor asked me the trouble and I said that the thought of losing all for which Devin had worked, obviously, gave him a despondency of the worst sort.

On this particular night, Willie, the bar keep at the "Bee", called in a panic.

"Mister Ryan, that brother of yours bought the whole house double Martinis and then he offered to take on any man, no matter what his height and girth."

"Well, how is he doing?" I asked.

"Fine. He felled poor Brendan Kelly, but Tim's waiting on line. Now, get yourself down here and be quick because I can't afford to have the house in shambles, Devin Ryan or not!"

I ran through the darkened Dingle streets to the "Bee" which was vibrating and banging with the interior struggle. A crowd was gathered about the outside window peering in towards the drunken gladiators. Devin was down on the floor wrestling Tim, the town strongman. As I peeled the bodies apart, someone ran in screaming,

"Mr. Ryan, Mr. Ryan. A warship has landed at your quay."

It was a general alarm. No warship had ever put into Dingle and I wondered if the man was not seeing things or had a few too many pints. As if shot from a gun, we ran towards the quay. Devin kept saying, "They're going to pay rent for dock space. That I promise." We came around the bakery side and soon we were joined by half the town running and stumbling over the wet cobbles. The party stopped fast against the wire gate to the quay.

Pressed to our dock, neatly snuggled, was a black submarine and we could see that she was rusted and covered in some places with weeds from the sea.

"I'll handle this, gentlemen. I'd like my vice-president to accompany me onto the quay," Devin said in the first bright tone that I had heard in weeks.

We moved through the gate and Tim, the bully, pleaded, "Mr. Ryan, I wonder if you would let us go, too?"

"Later, perhaps."

We walked slowly and cautiously. And there standing on the dock was a large thin man with a beard. A few other members of the crew stood on the conning tower. I remember one other thing—the submarine smelled. Yes, it had the stench of death or of unwashed bodies, or both. Devin walked up to the lone figure and extended his hand.

"I am Devin H. C. Ryan, President of the Ryan Brothers International Haulage and Warehouse Company, Incorporated."

He handed the officer a card.

"Ja," the officer said.

And then we knew.

"Permit me to introduce myself. I am Captain Hans von Holburg of the Imperial German Navy, Commander of the U-boat 197. I speak English, you see. In fact, most of the submarine officers are from excellent backgrounds."

Devin regarded the officer for a long while. The captain was unwashed and his blue coat was salted and wrinkled. But the man's smile was bright despite the dark circles beneath his eyes. He would have been a handsome warrior if he were clean and properly dressed.

"May I ask the purpose of your visit to our quay?" inquired Devin slowly.

"Indeed, Herr Ryan. We have a man aboard with acute appendicitis. I could not get him back to the pens at St. Nazaire. We had to put into a neutral country in the hope that the people would be good enough to save the man's life."

75

"I see," Devin said.

There was a lengthy pause.

"Well," Devin continued, "of course, we will take care of the man."

The captain looked at the fifty or so people straining against the fence.

"Are they friendly?"

"Of course."

"I wonder if I might buy a carton of cigarettes?" asked the officer.

"Naturally," Devin answered.

The captain shouted several orders to the men on deck and within a few minutes, the stricken sailor was lifted from the submarine and placed into the Rolls which Ronnie had brought to the quay as a matter of course.

"Ronnie, take this man to Doctor Kilmartin's," said Devin.

"He is lucky in a way. The war is over for him," the German said.

"Captain, why don't you come down to the office and we will have a drink and a cigarette together. If you don't mind, I would like to let the people on the quay see your U-boat. Most of them have never seen a submarine."

"Herr Ryan, first I must speak to you in confidence."

"You can speak in front of my brother."

"We have come off the Atlantic, Herr Ryan, after a difficult assignment. North Atlantic duty is not easy in winter, whether you are above the water or beneath it."

"I would not enjoy it," Devin said.

"The point is—we have expended our fighting capability. We are now going to France without offensive power. Dropping in here was dangerous. Would our presence here mean that someone in the village will call the British patrol boats and blockade our submarine in your harbour?"

"We guarantee absolute safety. You came here on a mission of mercy and our two countries are not at war."

The German captain passed a handshake towards Devin. At that point, we proceeded down the quay and Devin stood before the gate and began one of his commanding speeches.

"This is Captain von Holburg of the German Navy. The captain came to us because one of his men is dying with a terrible disease. I have directed one of my drivers to take the sick man to Dr. Kilmartin's. Captain von Holburg has kindly offered to let all of you take a close look at his submarine. But remember, he is our guest and we do not wish to make his presence known beyond the village. He tells me, off the record, that some people are not necessarily friendly to him and his country. So, we will keep things quiet."

A burst of laughter went up as Devin opened the gate. They wandered out along the quay to see the submarine with a kind of guilt. And that was the first of many steps.

THIRTEEN

By the time Devin and the U-boat skipper reached the office, they were smiling together as friends.

"Hans," Devin said, "you just sit down there in a chair and be comfortable while I pour out a large whiskey. How about a cigar?"

"Very kind of you, Devin. You have a wonderful office," the German said looking about.

"Thank you. We're in the haulage business. In fact, we have most of the market."

Devin served the drinks all around. The captain leaned back in the soft leather chair and raised his glass.

"Here's to a quick end of hostilities, Devin."

"Yes indeed," Devin answered. "I must show you our warehouse, Hans. We have the only cold-storage house in this part of Ireland."

Devin led the German into the warehouse which on that night was loaded with trans-shipments of meat and prod-

77

uce. I saw the German's eyes light up as he walked between the rows of hanging hams and beef sides. He stopped now and then to finger the meat. Two minds were beginning to click away and a broad smile came into Devin's face.

"This is a beautiful Limerick ham, Hans. Delicious. And here we have Bantry Bay prawns and shellfish just caught from the sea. Ah, none like it! Here are magnificent vegetables. Did you ever see a beet like this?" Devin asked, picking up the deep red vegetable.

The captain smelled the vegetable and I could feel the water rushing into his mouth.

"Over here we have fresh eggs and lamb ready for shipment. As you can see, we store whiskey in the unrefrigerated part of the warehouse, Irish whiskey and some American whiskey brought into Galway. We are the ones who transport most of the goods to the seaport."

"Yes! Yes!" the U-boat skipper said with new enthusiasm.

"I want to show you our beautiful beef. Look at those flanks, the cut of the ribs. That's solid, mouth-watering beef, Captain."

"Who gets all this beef, Devin?"

My brother thought for a minute and out came a claim which made me wince.

"Why, that's all going to the British Admiralty."

"The Admiralty," the captain said loudly, "they eat like that?"

"I believe it's going to the Admiral of the Fleet staff. Some of it is to be delivered to Churchill at 10 Downing Street. He loves ham for breakfast."

"Yes, I heard."

"The British consider that war should not necessarily cut off the good things in life," Devin said.

"Our supplies to the submarine service are of low grade. We found maggots in the bacon and the tinned goods are tampered with, I'm sure, by the French Resistance."

"That is a shame," Devin said. "I should think that you and your men would get the finest beef and ham for the sort of work you do."

"I think we should too, but that does not happen and I have inquired about it several times."

"It's still early. What about coming up to our house and having dinner and, perhaps, a nice hot bath?"

The German looked at Devin with longing eyes.

"We have to be out by daylight or before."

"But that gives us many hours. Please be our guest."

"I will accept your invitation, Devin. First, I must speak with my officers."

"Of course. You may invite them, too."

"No, I don't want to put you to that much trouble. But I will accept."

"Fine. We will leave for the house as soon as Ronnie gets back from the infirmary."

The German nodded his head and, as we retreated from the warehouse, his eyes were wider than ever as he inspected each ham and side of beef. Thoughts were lining up in his mind.

Mrs. O'Connor prepared a delicious steak dinner and Captain von Holburg told us in flourishing words of his life in prewar Germany—the opera, the cultured existence he enjoyed in Munich, the balls in Vienna.

"Yes, we enjoyed a gracious life much as you do, Devin. My father was a Munich businessman—exporting, importing. And I worked for the firm until I was pushed into this dreadful business of war."

"War is not designed for such men as you and me," Devin said.

"No, it is not! I agree. Shivering out there on the Atlantic, eating poor food, celled up in a U-boat. Ah, it is for fools!"

"What do you think of Hitler?" Devin asked slowly.

"He has a part of his brain missing. You might be interested to know, Herr Ryan, that in the German Submarine Service, we do not salute Hitler with 'heil'. That is how we feel. We honour the Fatherland, naturally. That is why we are fighting."

Devin went on to tell the captain of his problems with Hitler and the incident of the Rolls. The two of them seemed to get on from the very beginning because they both despised the Reichsführer.

"Do they give you the proper time off?" Devin asked further.

"No, it is tiring. We will put into St. Nazaire tomorrow afternoon. By next week we will go out again to hunt ships. I hate to live poorly and that is what I am doing. The other submarine officers feel the same way. War is uncomfortable. What else can we say about it? It is unnecessary and uncomfortable."

When Mrs. O'Connor brought the sherry, the captain became dead serious.

"Devin, I believe we are the same sort of men. We are both businessmen."

"I think we are alike in several ways," Devin answered.

"You are exporting your goods to England for the Admiralty, but they are not carried by your own ships."

"They are carried by English coastal steamers."

"I have seen these but we do not waste torpedoes on small coastal steamers. The point is, Devin, we are both engaged in the export business. Now my business has changed. I am trying to stop the export trade, as you can imagine."

He laughed and Devin joined in.

The captain went on, "What if we bought your hams and whiskey for the submarine service?"

There was a deathly silence in the room. I pressed my knees together and sweated somewhat under the arms. Devin, on the other hand, was thinking. I could tell when his mind was racing.

"Our prices are much too high. If we cut off supplies to our normal customers, we could never be sure of a constant market. As a businessman, captain, you must see the necessity of a constant market."

"I can supply a constant market."

"At our prices? Everything is so high."

"What is the price of your hams per pound?"

"Two pounds, eight."

I almost choked at that remark and I believe it was sent out by Devin as a joke since our hams were merely five shillings a pound.

"That *is* high," the U-boat captain said.

"Everything is high. We supply only top quality meats

80

and fish, those fine enough for the Prime Minister."

"I understand. Your meats are the best I have seen."

"Quality, captain, must be paid for, especially in wartime. You can imagine the economic situation. There are only so many grade A cuts of beef and they cost twenty times what the normal price would be."

"In Germany and France we receive very little ham, and I love pork. Scotch whiskey is hardly ever seen. The wines are poor, along with the meat. And, of course, cigarettes are very expensive if you can get them."

"You are asking me to sell you products?" Devin finally asked.

"That is what I am proposing. We have plenty of money in Germany and France, but nothing to buy. Money is not the problem. It is availability."

"Of course, of course. But I take a great risk in selling you products. There is nothing I cannot get, but what if the British found out I was diverting meat marked for the Admiralty to the German submarine service?"

"I am not asking you to refuel our submarines with oil or to store torpedoes. We are both businessmen, Devin, so it is rather obvious that we should start a venture between us. I have money. You have the goods, and I have the means of getting the supplies to our base in France. What difference does it make to the eventual outcome of the war if I eat your ham or our own tinned supplies?"

"About money," Devin said, "I'm not sure who is going to win at this point. Therefore, gold should be used as the coin of exchange."

"Naturally, we will win, Devin, and the German mark will be the standard of world trade. Our marks can be redeemed at the German Embassy in Dublin."

"Gold!" Devin demanded.

"You are a hard bargainer, Devin."

"Will you be exchanging goods on your own market in France and Germany? How will it operate?"

"There are many officers in the submarine service who are wealthy. They will pay almost anything for whiskey and good seasoned beef. Cigarettes will bring any price. The first step, as I see it, would be to take several of my fellow commanders into my confidence and, perhaps,

81

share the profits with them. As the U-boats come off the Atlantic on their way into St. Nazaire, they will have expended most of their fuel and torpedo loads. Therefore, we can haul thousands of pounds of goods back into France. That is, if you can get the merchandise for us."

"If the price is attractive, we will put all our vans at your disposal. When will you be passing Dingle again?"

"In about three weeks time."

"I shall then have a complete list of what we can offer you."

"A price list would help me. May I propose a toast to our mutual business venture, Devin."

The German rose to his feet and lifted his glass. My hand trembled as I held the glass high and saw the hard eyes of the captain through the liquid, his stiff jaw, his resolute smile. My God, here was the German Devin Ryan!

"And, Devin, if you will take German marks this time, I would like to relieve you of your entire supply of hams, cigarettes and whiskey to use as samples around the base."

"All right. We can even offer you American cigarettes."

"Do you have Lucky Strikes? I like that brand."

"I think we have Lucky Strikes and Camels, too. There is also a supply of Scotch."

The German looked at his watch and stiffened.

"Ah, the dawn will be here in two hours. I must clear the harbour in darkness."

As his words trailed off, the captain marched towards the door, bowing and thanking Mrs. O'Connor. We followed along, opened the warehouse, and under the cover of a misty darkness we loaded ninety hams, two hundred crates of canned goods, plus whiskey and cigarettes into the hot, cramped quarters of the submarine. The eyes of the crew lit up as they smelled the hams being pressed into the depths of their war machine. And when we stood in the interior light of the submarine, I saw the shocking horror of war—the sleeplessness hanging about their eyes, the dark circles on their gaunt white faces, the smell of unwashed bodies living in their cigar-shaped instrument of death.

What was the reason for this war? I am sure those on board that submarine had no idea. They were far removed from the plotting room of Hitler's brain and, too, their obsession and love for the Fatherland must have been mollified, if not eradicated, in that hell machine.

The hams and other supplies were settled inside the U-boat and we retreated to the dock watching them secure the hatches and start their deep-throated Diesel motors. The dock lines were slipped and she backed off as we walked along the quay with her until the rudders were put hard over, and the sub disappeared into the darkness of Dingle harbour.

I remember so well how we stood there watching this thing go as quietly as she came.

As the dawn was lighting Dingle, we sat in the office counting the marks and we saw that we had made on this some six hundred pounds clear profit. When we finished the accounting, Devin and I looked at each other and the hard reality of what had happened came upon us. We both felt the same sort of apprehension and uneasiness; I cannot say if it were a guilt because we were not sure a wrong had been committed.

"Now, Billy, I can guess what's in your mind. I'm wondering the same thing, too."

"Devin, we better stop this whole thing while we can."

"Is it wrong, Billy?"

"I think so. We are aiding the enemy."

"What enemy?"

"Well, the enemy of England. You yourself said that Hitler is a barbarian."

"But are we helping Hitler or a rather nice man who does not like the war?"

"Well, that nice man is torpedoing ships. That is the fact and he admits as much."

"What difference does it make if we supply him luxury goods? I imagine that the Swiss are still selling the Germans luxury goods. What about Portugal? They are still trading with the Germans."

"But, Devin, that is only rationalisation."

"Let's get to the facts, Billy. We're in trouble. I know it was my doing . . . . the way I spent money and went

83

on credit for everything, including the Rolls. I've made mistakes but now we're in trouble. You know as well as I that we can't supply the orphans with medicine if we don't pull some money in here. Oh, I should have thought of that before, so I know what you can rightfully say; but I've always been well intentioned. I've never hurt a soul. Now, I don't see how opening up a new market with the Germans for non-strategic items can possibly alter this war."

Devin was as tearful as he had been when he discovered his shot-up Rolls.

FOURTEEN

No one in Dingle knew that we had loaded the German submarine; and they did not realise, of course, what Devin had planted along the furrows of his brain. The full impact of this did not emerge until later that week. I was now convinced that supplying a few hams along the way and, perhaps, some cigarettes and fresh vegetables would not defy the code of international fair play.

"Why shouldn't we expand our export business to the Germans—in the area of non-strategic goods, of course," Devin said one morning. (Devin's own conscience was falling upon him and whenever he talked about goods, he always said "non-strategic goods".)

"I suggest," he stumbled on, "that we go to Dublin and procure samples of other products. Now, clothing is always a problem in wartime. People are cold, unable to buy blankets and sweaters, and the women, God bless them, are not able to get silk stockings or gowns, for that matter. And the people are unable to buy fine china or glassware. Think for a moment of the things we could offer our new clients. I say to you, we can open a department store right here in Dingle—beautiful gowns for the women, all sorts of china and items for the kitchen. Now, here is my plan. The submarine will be back in several weeks. When they return, the Ryan Brothers will be operating the finest shop in Ireland. I am going to Dublin to buy samples of everything. We will have a catalogue and take orders. Of course, we can sell the goods at ten times their worth. The important thing is that we display the merchandise well and put on a show when Captain von Holburg comes back into Dingle. He will understand the value of all this because I know he is a businessman able to see a profit for himself. What do you think of it, Billy?"

"Well . . . . I suppose . . . . it's fine." I really did not know what I was saying and the affirmation came almost mechanically.

"Then, it's settled. We leave for Dublin in the morning for a week's buying spree."

And it was a spree that I shall never forget. We bought out the silk stocking supplies of three shops and took back with us a sample of nearly every sort of consumer goods offered for sale in the Dublin markets. What we did not bring back we had in the way of a catalogue. Nothing was left out. By the end of that week, Devin was prepared to sell mattresses, chairs, fine antiques, silverware, diamonds, plus every tinned foodstuff imaginable. He also bought five mannikins and several boxes of ladies' undergarments. We set these up in the unrefrigerated section of the warehouse. The drivers for the firm poked their heads in now and then; of course, they did not quite understand what we were about as the bleak, functional warehouse took on the look of a Grafton Street department store. We even painted the floor and arranged beautiful lighting. All the while we were guarding against becoming too obvious in our sales approach. We wanted to suggest a bulk of available goods which had to be hidden because we were the exclusive proprietors. And, too, we wished to suggest that these goods were not really for sale, but in fact, on their way to England.

I never remember Devin as happy as he was during

85

those weeks. I was forced to pay the bills and keep an eye on the accounts which were dangerously low at this time. We had given up interest in almost every other area of our enterprise. The creameries were running themselves as always, but we did not go after new haulage business, hoping that our undersea trade routes would soon open. However, the orphanage was just about surviving. I decided not to wage a conflict with my conscience. I would simply wait and see what happened.

We had no idea really when the U-boat would come back from the North Atlantic patrol. For that matter, we were not assured it would ever reach us. I recall that one night I knelt beside my bed and prayed for the safe return of Captain von Holburg's submarine. If the U-197 failed to come back to Dingle, we were ruined. All of our cash reserves were expended for merchandise which, of course, we could not return.

The weeks trailed along and Devin became sullen. We posted a watch on the quay and one rainy night, we were called at our house.

"The warship's here," the voice said.

Devin and I jumped into the riddled Rolls and raced to the quay. It was about two o'clock in the morning, I remember, and there was the U-boat hawsered to our mooring bits. Again Captain von Holburg stood straight on the cobbles, his nut-brown beard a little longer, and his coat streaked with more salt trails. He looked tired, old and cold.

"Welcome, captain," Devin said. "Come on back to the office and have a warmth."

"I could use one, Devin," he said bleakly.

Captain von Holburg slipped into the soft leather chair and closed his eyes for a moment.

"Ah, this is an oasis."

"Please consider it a home away from home."

"I do. All the while we were out there I kept thinking of your warm office and the flow of your whiskey on my cold throat."

"Well, have some of that whiskey now. You must relax."

86

Devin handed the man a large glass of whiskey and he slipped lower in his chair. I felt that, perhaps, he was about to drift towards sleep.

"How is the war going, captain?"

"We got three ships, maybe another one."

My heart took an extra pound at the way the U-boat skipper said these things—matter of factly, without emotion.

"Is that a good run?" Devin asked.

"Not really. We expended all our torpdoes except one. We should have done better."

(I prayed to the saint of peace just then.)

"That must be trying for a man of your background and business sense," Devin said.

"Speaking of business, I have good news. Your hams were delicious. I am ready to place a full order."

The lights in Devin's eyes clicked on and I knew he was about to parade the exhausted captain into our department store.

"Since you were here last time, I have some new goods which we were lucky to get. Of course, they're going to the British."

"Don't keep threatening me with the British! They're too much of a threat already. A bother, really."

"I understand. But won't you come into the showroom, I mean, warehouse, to see our goods?"

We started back through the office and Devin snapped on the lights. The submarine captain was too exhausted to fully appreciate our wares, but Devin began one of his enthusiastic sales talks with the haggard German marching along behind.

"You see, captain, we have the finest hams and beef. As we move along, you will notice our new supply of goods, every conceivable kind of canned goods one could desire to make life a little easier in these terrible times."

"Very good," the captain said lighting his pipe.

"And now we step over to the cigarette counter. You will notice every possible brand of cigarettes, cigars and pipe tobacco. And now if you will follow me to the ladies' department. These, captain, are the finest women's

87

hosiery, silk, you know. Every woman wants silk stockings, something to keep the hearts of women going. And here we have ladies' finery."

Devin held up a delicate pair of feminine underwear, felt it gently and then looked over to the bras.

"These are the finest lace slips done in our own mills. The Irish are famous for lace. And now we arrive at the sweater counter . . . . handmade, every stitch turned by hand by the ladies in our cottages. These would keep anybody warm. Keeps cold out even on sub duty."

"Yes, yes," the captain said.

"Over here, you will see some glassware and silver, fine Waterford glass, makes anything taste better."

They went on to the vegetables lining the back of the warehouse.

"Here, look at the size of these young, crisp beets. Ever see anything like that, captain?"

"They are good beets, very good. I think I have seen enough. We will move to the office and talk," the captain said.

We settled again in the leather chairs. The German captain folded his hands and smiled at Devin.

"A very impressive show you put on for me. You are trying to sell me everything in Ireland."

"As a businessman, I am trying to show you what is available."

"Ja, ja, I appreciate that. As you know, we are occupying France, the centre of the women's fashion industry I am told. We have all the dresses we want. I would not be interested in all your goods put up so nicely for my benefit. I appreciate, nevertheless, good sales merchandising. I hope you will work for my firm after the war."

"Well, of course, no customer buys everything in the store."

"But let me tell you what I will buy. And I do not have gold but good German marks which can be turned in at our ministry in Dublin. I assure you they are as good as gold."

"I will trust you," Devin said, knowing that our first payment had been redeemed at the German Ministry in Dublin.

"The hams went over very well . . . . and the beef. I have the money to buy ninety sides of beef, seven hundred hams, all the cigarettes you have, the whiskey and the tinned goods, plus all the heavy wool sweaters and blankets. These things I can sell, not only to my fellow submarine men, but to other interested parties. I will pay your outrageous prices, Devin, if you will buy French perfume and French champagne at my prices. I know these things are *not* available in England and Ireland at the moment."

"If I can sell them," Devin said.

"I believe you are a merchant," the captain said coyly.

"But if I start marketing these goods, people will discover how I am getting the products."

"My dear fellow, you are so young. You will learn quick enough that no one questions where certain items come from in wartime. Questions like that are never asked."

"They will see you unloading your goods at the submarine base."

"Indeed they will. The commander, Admiral von Blitzman, has personally ordered my hams and Scotch. Please don't concern yourself with my end. But I do have a question. You see, Devin I have taken on several U-boats to act as cargo carriers along with my own. There will be sometimes two, sometimes five U-boats in here at one time picking up our cargo, if you can supply that many goods. I have written out the names of these men and the numbers of their boats. They might come in groups since the German Navy operates what we call "wolf packs". How are you to assure complete safety for my men and submarines? If the British discovered German submarines in here at night, they would throw a blockade around the port and take us in the morning. That would embarrass us."

"I should say, first of all, that no one in Dingle would call the authorities."

"I felt very confident last time."

"We could work out a signal device on the headland. Perhaps, a green light would be the signal that everything is in order and a red signal to say that trouble is around," Devin said in glee.

"Have English patrol boats ever come into Dingle?"

"They never have. Not *one* person was against your coming here last time."

"But that was to let off a dying man. When we arrive on a more frequent basis they will know that we are not dropping off sick seamen."

"Neither will they care."

"I hope you are right. We are taking a big risk."

"Absolutely no risk, captain. I assure you of that. You have the word of Devin Ryan and, as one businessman to another, I think you can rest easy on that."

"Let me put it to you another way. If the British blockade us in here some night, we shall be forced to shell the town. I say that, not as a threat, but only to show you that war is war."

"And business is business, so I shall safeguard that business relationship."

"Then, we understand each other."

"We do."

They shook hands.

"We only have a short time to load. My second officer will start while you make up a bill. I also have some goods for you which we will take off the bill. The next time, I believe I should arrange things differently. We had a lot of trouble on our patrol. I found several of my men drinking the elixir with breakfast and using the perfume as shaving lotion. In fact, our submarine still smells like a whorehouse. The next time, I will deliver my goods on the way from St. Nazaire and pick up your supply on the way in."

"That is quite all right," Devin said, smiling to his ears.

"I also have the list for next time. You can expect my pick-up submarines to be in during the early part of next week. They know the harbour and you will have the signal placed on the headland."

The quay came alive. The whole crew of the sub emptied out and the crates were loaded down through the open hatches. There was shouting of orders in German as the cases were hauled from our warehouse. I did get a chance to go below and all available space was jammed with goods; there were hams in the captain's cabin, sides of beef in the alleyways, vegetables and sweaters in the engine room, cases of whiskey piled high and secured inside the conning tower, cases of cigarettes in the torpedo tubes and several boxes of ladies' underwear on the deck of the control room. We unloaded sixteen cases of French champagne and eleven boxes of perfume. Then we settled the accounts and the Germans gave us wads of money tied in brown string. Devin said it came to about four thousand pounds. The pace picked up suddenly; the lines were slipped and the sub backed from our quay. Devin waved to Captain von Holburg on the conning tower and he, in turn, flashed a knowing, informal salute back at my brother.

A lump still rested in my throat. It was attached to some fear and perhaps some guilt, and I could only hope that Mother Mary Rose and Father Dunn were not looking upon this scene. I knew there would be a whole new confrontation when those two were finally aware of our new benefactor.

FIFTEEN

Besides the initial payment, our German friend in commerce gave us an additional four thousand pounds to fill his new order which, at that point, seemed to represent the entire beef, ham, whiskey and cigarette supply in Ireland. In a sense, we were fully committed to this undersea trade. I secretly feared that if we stopped now, this man would simply destroy the town. He appeared to be reasonable, not really the villain as depicted by postwar motion pictures on the theme. But as he said himself, "War is war." I certainly did not wish to have the blood of an entire village on my hands, but the wrestling I did with my conscience was not acute until that day I went out to Dunmore Head.

I spoke with a Mrs. Rafferty who owned about the only house on that wind-blown headland. Her husband had died. (All Irish husbands seem to die early; that is one of the reasons I have never taken a wife.) The widow was ageless and wrinkled deeply by the gales which blew against her exposed perch. The house was of one storey, built of stuccoed brick and slated on top. Of course, there was no electricity or telephone and she lived a barren existence; her sustenance came from a government pension and the sale of wool from the sheep I saw roaming before her place. While Devin and our drivers were off collecting meat for the orders, my job was to find a house where we could hang the red and green signals. I did not quite know how to handle this delicate situation. (One never knew who was for whom in this country of mixed angers and sudden emotions.) I knocked on the door and the Widow Rafferty opened it wide to admit me.

"Now, isn't that a fancy motorcar," she said, looking at the damaged Rolls.

"I'm Billy Ryan from the village."

"I thought you might be Devin Ryan. I hear a lot about that young man."

"He wanted to come himself but he is out of town on business."

"And what would you be wanting up here on the Head?"

Her direct question threw me off because I was planning to soften her a bit and then move on to the matter at hand.

"Well, you see, Mrs. Rafferty, we were wondering . . . . I mean, my brother, Devin, was wondering . . . . if you would help us."

"How can a poor woman like me help you two?"

"It has been brought to the attention of my brother that we do not, I mean, the government has not given proper lights for fishing vessels to enter the harbour. Devin has taken it upon himself to set up a navigational system since the government will not accept the responsibility."

92

As I spoke, my mouth was drying quickly and I believe she realised this because a sceptical look was on her face. It was difficult to tell if she were smiling or whether the wrinkles merely made her mouth appear that way.

The sudden shock, however, one which I felt from the top of my eyebrows all the way to my toes, was the sound of my own voice. I was becoming another Devin and I was not so sure I needed that.

". . . . We can thank God that there is one man in Dingle who takes it upon himself to assure the safety of the fishermen."

"So, you want to buy my land for a lighthouse. Would you come in and have some tea?" she inquired brightly.

My mouth dropped open as she rushed me inside the neat cottage and began boiling water for tea.

"You know, this is the highest land on the coast. I can see all the way out and watch the ships go by at sea. Your brother is being wonderful and generous by opening a lighthouse to protect mariners. But I do not like the idea of moving into the village. Our family has occupied this land for seventy years. For an old woman to take new roots is hard, Mr. Ryan."

"No, no. I don't mean to suggest that we want to move you."

"Then, how could you be building a proper lighthouse on the headland? This house occupies the highest spot."

"We were thinking of something on a smaller scale."

"How much less?" she snapped.

"You see, we wanted to begin in a modest way, to test the light. We don't know which colours will be best. But as an experiment, we would hang lanterns in the window by night. Most of the time, green—and, then, sometimes perhaps a red lantern. You could be the light station tender and earn extra money. How would you like that?"

"What would you pay? I am very poor and it will take time to keep the light in working order."

"We could start with a pound a week."

"Lighthouse keepers get more than that, Mr. Ryan."

"But they are paid by the government."

"You have given me an idea. Maybe I will write up to Dublin and suggest my land for a proper lighthouse."

"No, no," I said quickly. "My brother wishes this to be his own project, a surprise for the government. How would three pounds a week be? Would that be to your liking?"

"It might be."

"Then I will buy two lanterns, red and green. Every night you will put the green lantern in your window unless we come up and tell you to display the red light."

"I would like an advance, Mr. Ryan."

"Oh yes, here's the first week's wage, three pounds."

"The price might go up considerably if I find that the light keeps me awake."

"I'm sure it will not."

"This is a responsibility, Mr. Ryan."

"Yes, it is. You're right about that," I gulped, "a very large responsibility."

I stood there a minute and wondered if we had another version of Devin Ryan around Dingle, and she said slyly, "These light signals can be seen by U-boats, can they not, Mr. Ryan?"

My heart almost leaped out of my chest.

"I . . . . ah . . . . we don't have . . . . what did you call them?"

"Submarines, Mr. Ryan."

"Oh, submarines. If there were submarines around here, I suppose they would see the light. But I don't know of any submarines around Dingle."

She took me by the hand and we walked outside her house and through the tufts of grass to the cliff edge. She pointed far down to the rock masses lying like scattered bits of coal around the base of the Head. And the horror of this agony upon the sea came back to me in a fresh way. Upon the rocks, sprinkled like matchsticks, were a battered lifeboat and wooden crates spewing their contents all over the slime-green boulders.

"What do you suppose caused that wreckage, Mr. Ryan, but U-boats?"

My heart raced with relief. I had thought she was onto our trading. And then I said a stupid, mindless thing.

"Maybe that is wreckage from a German U-boat."

"Submarines do not carry lifeboats, Mr. Ryan."

94

"That's right," I said quickly, trying to laugh off my mistake. "But submarines don't come in this close or cause damage to shipping around here. Have you ever seen a ship sunk out there?" I asked.

"I have never seen a ship sunk, true enough. But I have seen a submarine."

"When was that?"

"The morning before last. I get up with the dawn. And I was out on the Head collecting eggs from my chickens when I happened to look up as the light was just filling the sky."

"Go on, go on. What did you see, Mrs. Rafferty?"

"I looked out and there was a long black shape, about two miles off, sailing as nice as can be into the morning light. At first I couldn't imagine what it could be, but right before my eyes, it gets smaller and smaller and it finally just went underneath the sea. Well, my first thought was to race for the village and call the Bantry lifeboat. Was it a ship that just sank before my very eyes? Then, I realised it was an undersea boat, Mr. Ryan, an undersea boat."

"Maybe your eyes were playing tricks," I said with a false smile.

"Go on with you. My eyes are good. I tell you, I saw a U-boat, a German U-boat. As best as I could make out, she came right out of Dingle harbour. Imagine that!"

"Very strange."

"I wonder if it was strange or if it was not so strange at all," she said, eyeing me now.

"It could have been an English U-boat. The English have submarines."

"An English submarine in an Irish port? Nonsense! I think this was a German underwater boat. I've been reading about these things in the paper."

"I don't think we'll ever know," I said, shaking my head.

"Yes, we will, Mr. Ryan. I will tell you why. When I went into Dingle just yesterday for flour, I stopped into Michael's grocery shop and there was some talk in the place that a German submarine had come into the harbour to let off a sick man."

"Well than," I said with a spirit of joy, "don't you see, that explains it."

"What does it explain?"

"They came back for the sick man and picked him up. That's how it was."

"They did not. I asked about the sick man and he went off to Dublin almost a fortnight ago."

"But the Germans didn't know that, so they came back to fetch him."

"Mr. Ryan, I've been down to the quay. Mr. Devin Ryan owns the quay and the house at the end of the quay."

"The company owns the premises, yes."

I knew this shrewd little woman, this fertile leaping mind, had stumbled onto the truth of the matter. And I put my hands into my pockets and just waited for her to reel off the entire facts.

"These lights, Mr. Ryan, they are to help the German U-boats come into Dingle, aren't they now?"

"They are," I sighed.

"Green means come straight ahead. Red means stay back?"

"Yes, Mrs. Rafferty," I mumbled.

"What are you selling them, torpedoes and oil?"

"Of course not. My brother and I are exchanging hams, cigarettes and beef, some sweaters, too—we are trying to support the nuns as best we can."

"They're buying sweaters?" she asked brightly.

"Yes, Mrs. Rafferty. Only non-strategic goods. Nothing which can hurt anyone unless you believe that a well-fed German skipper is more dangerous than one who is carrying a knot in his stomach.

"Mr. Ryan, I knit very well and I know plenty of ladies who can knit beautiful sweaters."

"Then, it's settled. We will put you in charge of the knitting department and pay you a top price. You can also work the lighthouse. How would you like that?"

"Maybe. It's lonely up here on the Head."

"When my brother comes back from his business trip, I will have him see you and we can set up the wage."

"And, Mr. Ryan, many of my lady friends bake won-

derful cakes and delicious pies. I want them in on this
business relationship."

"Well, Mrs. Rafferty, let's start with the signal lights,
then we can talk about the sweaters, cakes and pies. And
please do not tell anyone about this."

"Not a word to anyone," she said, holding her finger to
her mouth. "Not a word from my lips."

I backed away realising then that the whole of Dingle
would know about our dealings within the week if they did
not know already. But we could use these ladies as our
front. I knew Devin would be delighted to hear the outcome of the events on Dunmore Head.

SIXTEEN

The waterway of slightly shaded commerce, we were to
find, was tormented by gales of the worst description.
Running a string of creameries and carting produce about
in our lorries did in no way qualify us for the shrewder,
harsher world of international trade, especially an underwater enterprise with an anxious nation. I believe
Devin realised the portent of darkish clouds when he came
back into Dingle after buying every ham and beef side in
the western countryside of Ireland. It was early December
by that time and the Atlantic was sending us furious rain
for weeks on end. Devin no longer wore his three-piece
suit or talked about the latest article in *Fortune* magazine;
he was now bruising his nose on the wheel of a delicate
grindstone—insurrection!

Yes, that is what he called it. "The nerve of the people
around me!" he said in one of his stormiest outbursts.

(Devin believed, in some grand twist of his thinking,
that he alone could be the arch opportunist in these grave

times. He could not ascribe that tendency to anyone else, except for the German who had exhibited that enterprising flare to keep Ryan Brothers International "international".)

All these blasts fell on Devin the night he arrived. I never saw my brother quite so tired or depressed by the state of things. Two of his vans had broken down on the road; another had flattened nine sheep just outside Kilkenny. He recovered from the latter by purchasing the carcasses for a future lamb sale, even though these were wool-bearing old sheep, much too tough to eat even for hardy submariners.

He came into the office about half-two in the morning. I had stayed up since he rang through from Tralee saying that we must have an emergency meeting. There was more of an emergency than he realised.

Mrs. Rafferty got to thinking and turned out to be the thorniest bargainer of all. She organised every lady in the town and already they were baking hundreds of cakes, pies, breads and delicate desserts. Women who had never knitted in their lives were pressed into service; soon every lady for miles around was busy with needles, dropping stitches, mixing patterns and, generally, turning out the worst "Irish-type" sweaters I had ever seen—and my eye is not practised at evaluating knitting. Besides that, their cakes were collapsing and sour to the taste. Mrs. Rafferty demanded that I buy these for the right to display the green signal in her window. It was, no doubt, extortion, a conspiracy of the boldest sort. When I told the woman she had to wait for our president to return, she took this as a literal suggestion and remained at the warehouse day and night with several ladies at her side comforting her and saying that the skinflint, Devin Ryan, better get back into the town or else!

It was the "or else" which gave a severe shiver to my stomach making the juices pour out of the wrong ducts, so that I could only take tea and honey. I imagined how the irate U-boat captain would swing his deck gun over Dingle; perhaps he would send his men ashore to line every one of us up along the wall of the church. Lord help us! That is all I could say. I fully realised that Mrs. Rafferty and her women could call the British Consulate in Dublin, and the British patrol boats would block off Dingle harbour trapping the Germans along our quay. And would the British come to defend us when the U-boats turned against the town? The bloody hell they would! Why should they defend a country who refused to side with them as allies?

As Devin walked in, dripping and unshaven, Mrs. Rafferty and her ladies grabbed him by the arm.

"So you're the big president we've been hearing about. We want our money and be quick!"

"What the devil is this?" Devin shouted, pulling away from their grasp.

"We've been working our fingers to the bone, Mr. Ryan, and several ladies burned their hands slaving over a hot stove for you."

"Get them out of here," he yelled, moving to his bar for a quick bracer.

"Devin, come into the office and I'll explain everything. Ladies, we must have a meeting. Mr. Ryan will see you in a short time. Just wait out here."

I pushed Devin inside the door and locked it.

"Why in the name of the saints must I come home to this after such a trip?"

"Devin, we might as well face a few things right now. This new expansion programme of ours is going to cause trouble."

"Trouble? What do you think I've been having all week? I can hardly get rid of the champagne, the German Embassy is asking questions about the money exchange and no one wants that lousy French perfume. What the hell does the German think this country is! We don't have women who use perfume."

"There must be someone who uses perfume," I asserted weakly, looking into the fiery, black eyes of the harassed company president.

"Irish women don't use it the way French women do. Why can't our women have sex on the mind? We're a sexless race, Billy. We might as well face that as part of our legacy. I don't even think we're a country of bathers."

"There's very little hot water in Ireland."

Devin slumped behind his desk and buried his moist forehead in his hands.

"Who is this Mrs. Rafferty?" he said under his breath.

"She's going to be one of our problems. I went up to Dunmore Head as you asked and talked Mrs. Rafferty into being our lighthouse keeper."

"What about the cakes or whatever it is?"

"The truth is, Devin, she saw the U-boat going out last week. When I came in asking to put a green lantern in her window, she worked the whole thing out. I ran into a thinker by mistake."

"You're bloody right it was a mistake. So, she's putting extortion on us, blackmail and insurrection?"

"I had to tell her what we were doing. She didn't react one way or the other, even when I mentioned the nuns. But she *did* feel she could organise the ladies of Dingle into a trading company of their own."

"How?" Devin demanded.

"About two hundred women started baking cakes for the submarine men. Others began on sweaters, They delivered four hundred tins of baked goods yesterday. They stood in line and I had to pass out credit slips and congratulate them on their work. Well, that was the wrong thing to do because they're out baking more cakes."

"Oh, God, how much do I owe them?"

"Almost two hundred pounds for the cakes and a hundred and fifty pounds for the sweaters. The cakes are terrible and the sweaters worse."

"Well, Billy, you just better figure out some way to pay them."

"We don't have the money, Devin. I told them the Germans were bringing in the money."

Just as I finished the explanation, the door shook with hard knocks. I opened it slowly and the women spilled into the office.

"Ladies, ladies, Mr. Ryan is planning to honour your good efforts."

The light came upon Devin and he rose to his feet with a genuine boyish smile gliding into his weary face.

"I am proud of every one of you," he said, "very proud

that each of you has become a supplier to the Ryan Brothers International. And God in heaven will certainly bless you for helping the sick orphans over at St. Ann's. I am truly sorry that I could not taste your cakes individually."

"Would you like a nice piece, Mr. Ryan?" Mrs. Rafferty said with warmth in her words.

"Not just now, thank you. But I will, I will. My brother says he received your cakes and gave you credit notes. I have something better, much better."

"Better than money?" one of them asked.

"We happen to have some very expensive perfume direct from France, the kind of perfume that the beautiful international French ladies wear. I am going to announce a dividend—a bottle for each lady who has given her time and talents to our company. Will you distribute the perfume, Mrs. Rafferty . . . . I think it is?"

She blushed and said, "God bless you, Mr. Ryan. You are a fine man."

"Thank you. It came from the best shop in Dublin. We're exporting it to France, you know, but I will divert that shipment, make the French women wait."

The ladies giggled, not catching the swift ways of Devin's mouth—the fact that he was exporting French perfume to France. Victorious and still carrying his smile, Devin rang the inside warehouse.

"Ronnie, Mr. Ryan here. You know that perfume, the very expensive brand, the five-pound kind? Yes, the perfume we're exporting to French stores. Please stop the processing and bring a few crates in here."

Devin put down the phone and a short time later, Ronnie and two men came through the door hauling the half opened crates.

"Look at that, ladies. Imagine, French perfume!"

He bent down and opened a bottle smearing a little on the wrist of Mrs. Rafferty. She brought the wrist to her nose in a burst of small laughs.

"Oh, it smells wonderful, Mr. Ryan."

"Now, you may take these bottles and we'll have more by tomorrow if you will stop around."

"Thank you. We'll have more cakes, too."

101

Oh, Lord, I thought to myself.

"Mrs. Rafferty, about the cakes . . . we don't know when our . . . er "trading ships" will come. They're on an irregular schedule because of other matters."

"Like the war?" Mrs. Rafferty said, lifting her knowing face.

"It has something to do with the war effort. What I was going to say is this. We shouldn't bake too many cakes because they might go stale and we wouldn't want that, would we?"

"But they're all sealed and tinned. They'll remain fresh for weeks."

"Just concentrate on the sweaters until further notice," Devin said firmly. "Ladies, that will be all."

The women picked up the small bottles and they went out into the rain titillated and chattering.

We drank that night, the two of us, until the rain lightened into a gloomy grey—the start of another miserable Dingle day.

SEVENTEEN

Just as we were getting the accounts in order and preparing for the German undersea fleet, another delegation appeared at the warehouse demanding to see Devin Ryan. Their spokesman, Tim O'Rourke, as muscular between the ears as he was on his forearms, marched into Devin's sanctum carrying all the odours of the "Bee". I knew that this plot had been hatched in the bar room and from there the delegation, some twenty-five of them, brought their stout-drooling mouths into our office full of greed, and thirsty for an easy pound. They gathered about Devin's desk, all of them holding rumpled caps in their hands, and

I am sure they felt a little ashamed of their proposals. Tim, in his coarse, pitted voice, delivered the thoughts of the others.

"Devin, we've been patient with you."

"Patient. Why patient?"

"With all your fancy cars and running the dock, trying to charge the mackerel men fees and the like."

Devin tapped his pencil on the table and then delivered a curt order.

"Tell me what you want. Say it! Then get out!"

"We'll say it. You've turned this town into a prime target for British bombers and you've endangered our lives and ruined our homes. None of us has anything to eat these days because the stoves are busy with cakes. And our women don't mind us anymore. They're all working for you."

"For money," Devin broke in, "for the old pound."

"For cheap perfume. Our houses all smell like flower gardens and some of us are sick to the stomach because our women are parading about like show girls."

"Is that all?" Devin asked slowly.

"You can't be ruining this town, taking our women away from their jobs and turning the place into a German naval base."

"Do the Germans fire cakes through their torpedo tubes?" Devin asked.

"We don't want our homes destroyed because of your bargaining. We are the ones who will suffer while you collect the pounds."

"Now the truth comes out! Go on."

"Well, if we could take a part of the profits, we'd take the risks and allow our women to work for you."

"Are you organising a union along with your wives?"

"You might be calling it that," Tim said.

"And I suppose you've drawn up a list of wage demands?"

"That we have."

Tim pulled a crumbled piece of brown paper from his inside coat pocket and passed it to my brother. As Devin read the outrageous working agreement—triple time for loading the submarines at night—he boiled with an anger

103

that almost made him split at the temples.

"Go to hell! Every one of you."

"Our women will stop working for you."

"I don't need their terrible cakes."

"And when those subs come in, we're going to block the harbour mouth with fishing trawlers. And then, by God, we'll call the British people in Dublin and there'll be no lantern in Mrs. Rafferty's window!"

"Let me tell you something and hear it well. Devin Ryan is not to be threatened. I have sacrificed for this town, tried to bring commerce here in the best way I could, and we have nuns and orphans to feed. If you call the British or block the Germans in this harbour, you'll be sporting two enemies. The Germans will shell the town, level it to dust, mind you! Every one of you will perish—men, women and children! So think again about threatening me."

They shuffled out, never looking back at Devin, who seemed to be the winner. But it was not a victory because they were obviously going back towards the "Bee" to regroup for another assault.

EIGHTEEN

Miss Tremble who always arrived from her quarters at Brenner's Hotel at precisely half-eight came in on this particular morning at ten minutes to the hour of nine. Now Devin and I were trying to pull ourselves into shape for the day since we had spent most of night drinking and talking over incidents from our childhood. (It was one of the few times I can recall my dear brother sitting down and relaxing enough to speak of things that had no practical matter.) At any rate, we had shaved quickly in the small bathroom hoping that Miss Temple would not see and smell the evidence of what we had been up to. Her lateness helped but we saw in her eyes a frostiness, and Devin and I crossed looks as we greeted her. She went to her typewriter, pulled off the cover, pretended to look at one of the keys and, then, sniffing as she went, Miss Tremble walked briskly into Devin's office with a harder than usual lip circling her face as if it had been pencilled on.

"Mr. Ryan, it is time that we discuss a serious point," she started, smelling the air once again.

"Of course, anything, Miss Tremble," Devin said.

"There has been no one in this Godforsaken town that has appreciated your youth, enthusiasm and vigour more than I. I think you will appreciate the point that it was I, above everyone else, who sensed the worldliness and atypical Irishness of your activities."

"Of course, Miss Tremble. I realise your faithfulness."

"And when you called that night with the idea of bringing the orphans over here, I actually said to Father Dunn when he came around, 'Devin Ryan has some saintliness in him'."

"Thank you, Miss Tremble."

"Your thoughtfulness in sending a jelly here or there to honour somebody's birthday showed that you cared. And I add, Mr. Ryan, that no one pitched in to settle those children more than I did. I scrubbed the floor of that warehouse myself so the children could have a place when they arrived."

"Yes, yes, Miss Tremble. What are you getting at?"

Just then, her slanty eyes grew round and wetness came into them. Soon she was crying and then hysteria came over the woman. Devin raced for a glass of water and when we settled her down a bit, she continued, interrupting her words now and then with huge, choking sounds.

". . . . My sister, Gladys . . . . Gladys Tremble, a fine maiden lady from Aston Clinton, a woman who has given her whole life to the community as town librarian, joined the Royal Air Force."

(Devin and I immediately thought that Miss Tremble's

maiden sister might have been gunned down on the flightline.)

". . . . And Gladys is now risking her life to help England win this horrible war."

"Miss Tremble, I am delighted that your sister is joining the effort," I said.

"Is she training to be a ferry pilot or an auxiliary?" Devin asked.

"She is not," Miss Tremble said with a tone of pride on her voice. "My sister has taken over the library at the Oxbury Fighter Base, giving those poor boys the right books to read for their only enjoyment."

"Oh, how courageous of her," Devin said, trying to sound sincere.

It was on those words that Miss Tremble broke down. "How could you, Mr. Ryan?" she said again through her tears. "How could you!"

"How could I what, Miss Tremble?"

"Can't you see? My sister is risking her life as an R.A.F. librarian right on the aerodrome, doing her job fighting Hitler, and her God-given sister is helping Germany. I am really at war with my sister!"

"Oh God," Devin sighed. "I'll never last."

"What am I to tell my sister in our letters . . . . that I am over here in Ireland loading U-boats? How can I keep my head up when I'm involved in this anti-English effort?"

Devin rose to his feet and moved around the room, his head bowed as if deep in painful thought.

"I understand, Miss Tremble. I understand. But you know the accounts around here. You see our ledgers. Where do you think the money from the German submarine trade is going?"

"I realise that it is being directed to the nuns for a very worthy cause."

"And do you realise that we are not giving the enemy strategic goods?"

"I have thought of that for nights now. I have not taken an hour's sleep since this dreadful thing happened. But, Mr. Ryan, you are aiding the enemy because you are comforting them."

"You must remember that Ireland is not at war with Germany."

"I personally cannot have a sister risking her life on an R.A.F. station and in good conscience be over here helping to feed the German Navy. . . . orphans or no orphans."

"And would you wish the little children to starve?"

"The end in this case does not justify the means. I am resigning, Mr. Ryan."

"Miss Tremble, you can't," Devin pleaded.

"I must. I am taking up a position as a special food adviser to the Royal Navy. I shall be working with the Ministry of Supply seeing to it that the best use is made of the sea stores."

"I wish you all the luck, Miss Tremble, and I hope you do not think I am against an English victory."

She broke down in tears again and we could not understand why until she said, "And a group of us will be going to sea as observers to improve galley procedures on small craft."

"You are going to sea, Miss Tremble?" I asked.

"Yes, and I might be torpedoed by one of the submarines that you are supplying," she sobbed.

"I'll never last," Devin said again.

At the end of those words, Miss Tremble stood up and said, "God Save the King." She shook our hands formally and left the office and our employ forever.

Devin seemed to take the blow quite in stride, sympathising with Miss Tremble to a point. But her sentiments brought home to us the risks we were taking. I think at that point we came very close to calling a halt to the whole trading affair. Perhaps we would have reconsidered if Mother Mary Rose had not appeared at the office that morning, not one hour after Miss Tremble delivered her sentiments.

"Good Morning, Mother Mary," Devin said, trying to cover his breath. "Won't you be seated? And what a bright morning it is."

"Yes, but my heart is down, Devin."

"What could be the problem? I thought everything was going fine at the orphanage."

"It is. The children are so happy. You know, we get them out much more than we did in London."

"Fine. Fresh air cures all sorts of things. I think I'll be taking more long walks in the open air. I have high blood pressure, you know, from working so hard."

"Oh, Devin, you must care for yourself. You look so white this morning."

"Particularly bad night with all the accounts."

Mother Mary smiled sympathetically. (Amid all the confusion of bringing ourselves into the submarine trade, the problems of inventorying the goods and the local rebellions, Devin had made it a rule that no one in the town should discuss the U-boat affair with Mother Mary. Our only fear at this time was Father Dunn. He had remained strangely quiet. Father obviously knew what was going on and the first confrontation with the man would decide many things. However, everyone in the village pledged his solemn word not to tell the Reverend Mother or her nuns that Devin was trading internationally. I am sure if she discovered the true source of her funds, she would be stricken with conscience and embarrassment.)

"Oh, it's a hard thing I have come to talk about," she said.

Devin looked frightened and he sat down behind his desk quickly waiting for the fateful words.

"I know how generous you have been, Devin, moving us here, offering us the new orphanage. But last year we were promised new whirlpool baths and rehabilitation equipment by the London bishop. This was to cost three thousand pounds. I'm afraid we cannot do very much for these poor children without modern equipment. I thought I would bring the problem to you."

"Well . . . . you see, Reverend Mother, the war is on and to come by such equipment would be impossible."

"I have discovered some physiotherapy equipment in Cork at the cost of two thousand pounds. Many of our children are at that age where their whole usefulness as adults will depend on what rehabilitation we give them at this point. Doctor Hawkins claims that we should employ a therapist also."

"And what does that cost?" Devin asked.

"About twelve pounds a week for a good one. I'm so embarrassed to be coming around and asking for these things."

"Well, Reverend Mother, I'll try to pass the hat to several foreign friends who stop by every now and then."

"Are they influential people?"

"Why yes, they are exerting quite an influence on the world these days," Devin said, biting into his words with a cough.

"You do have such fine friends," our aunt added, "and I hate to impose on your guests. Would it help if I spoke to your friends? I could tell them about our needs or they could come up to St. Ann's and see for themselves."

"No. You see, Reverend Mother, my business friends only come in late at night after your bedtime, I'm sure. And they stay but a few hours. They are very busy men."

"God bless you, Devin. God bless you. I just said to Father Dunn the other day what a saintly person you are."

"Ah, Mother Mary . . . . ah, I haven't seen Father Dunn for weeks now. How did he seem? Did he say anything about me or Billy?"

"Oh no. He said he was working on his trains, keeping his mind off problems."

"Problems?" Devin asked.

"I suppose the poor man is lonely up there in the parochial house. We try to have him visit us to see the children every day."

"Good. Very good. By the way, your nuns don't usually go out on the roads at night, do they?"

"We never leave the orphanage after nightfall."

"Splendid," Devin said, rubbing his hands together.

"Why do you ask?"

"Well . . . . ah . . . I've heard that a wild, drunken driver comes over from Tralee every night and races his motor car up and down these roads. They say he has killed many sheep along the Connor Pass. We wouldn't want you or your nuns run down after dark. So, just stay in the orphanage until they arrest this man."

"Of course, Devin. I will tell everyone including Doctor Hawkins not to go out after dark. And thank you in advance for whatever you can do for us."

109

Devin showed Mother Mary to the door. As we opened it, there was a picket line in front of the warehouse. Men and women marched up and down with signs saying such things as:

DEVIN RYAN UNFAIR TO THE
WOMEN KNITTERS
ARE WE BAKING FOR HITLER
OR DEVIN?
MORE MONEY TO LOAD THE
U-BOATS

"Labour trouble, Devin," I said.

"Oh God, this is just what we need."

"Why are they marching in front of the door carrying signs about Hitler?" Mother Mary asked.

"It's just one of those things, Mother Mary. You go along to the orphanage and I'll talk to them."

There was some shouting, cat calls at Devin, and then my brother caught hold of the Reverend Mother's stole and yelled to the crowd, "Reverend Mother, tell these good men and women of Dingle what you were just talking to me about!"

"The orphanage is in need of more funds. And Mr. Ryan has pledged his help."

The peaceful look of the nun seemed to quiet everyone. She smiled and walked past them up the road towards the orphanage.

We let their spokesmen into the office and decided upon a set of working conditions for loading and unloading the submarines. Along with this, there was to be a wage control and price set-up for the products of the town: single layer cake would bring, for instance, eleven shillings; a pie, eight shillings; a turtle neck sweater, two pounds four; tinned vegetables, depending upon size, from two shillings up to four shillings.

And so that day we became a unionised shop. Of course, we did not approach the closed shop modus with a formal labour-management contract; it was only a written agreement but quite specific. Well, the union rejoiced all

110

that day and through the night. Something had been put over on the shrewd Devin Ryan. It was well worth it, though, because the dangers of insurrection and irritating the Germans were over. The lantern went back into Mrs. Rafferty's window; cakes were baked; sweaters were finished and our two-man vans rolled about southern Ireland picking up the last bits of beef and pork.

NINETEEN

It was warm in the weeks before Christmas of that year. Devin and I took to walking the roads near Dingle. We did not say too much to each other on these strolls; often I would be seeing my brother from the corner of my eye as we went. His thoughts seemed to be settled on some far off idea. It was not so much a scheme, but a terrible wrangling which was going on inside of him. I knew that Devin was becoming nervous over what had been created. The fact that we had never directly confronted Father Dunn in all of these months left both of us to do some deep thinking.

It was almost dusk as we walked on this one December night. A smell of French perfume hung in the air and all the cottages were sending up curls of blue-grey smoke; we knew there was a cake in each of the ovens (and the clicks of knitting needles could almost be heard).

We were in our thoughts and, suddenly, there was a shrill bell behind us. Turning, we saw Father Dunn coming towards us on his bicycle. He stopped and the meeting was not in the least sharp or unfriendly.

"How are you getting on, Father?"

"Well enough, Devin. And yourself?"

"I've been very busy with things," my brother said.

Father Dunn was off his bike now and he pushed it

111

along with us taking in the night air. None of us knew how to break the awkward silence or just what to say. The road came past our house and Devin asked Father Dunn if he would not like to stop in for a sherry. Mrs. O'Connor greeted us at the door and when she saw Father standing there with his bike, she flashed a shocked look towards Devin. (There was not a person in Dingle, except the nuns and perhaps their befuddled staff physician, who did not wonder when Devin Ryan was to come face to face with Father Dunn.) The meeting was so long delayed that some of the men were taking bets down at the "Bee". I do suppose that everyone wished for a stormy confrontation; there were those who said that conflict would reach the boiling point at mass some Sunday. A few claimed that Father Dunn was about to leave Dingle.

But Father simply came in, loosened his Roman collar, and looked at the rheostat for the central heating as Uncle Shemas had done in years past. When he was settled in the study, Father happened to glance about and see the piles of unopened magazines resting in the corner.

"Haven't been reading lately, Devin?"

"No, I haven't, Father," Devin said.

And then, Devin reached under his desk and came up with a box in a Christmas wrapping. He walked towards Father and handed him the parcel.

"It's a bit early for Christmas, Father, but I thought I would give this to you now."

"Why, thank you, Devin. Feels heavy."

Father opened the wrapping and then the box. He pulled from it a steam model shunting engine. Father looked at it closely and then towards Devin.

"You didn't have to do this, Devin."

"I thought you would enjoy it."

"Oh, Devin . . . . you don't have to buy me off anymore as you did by putting the second track in my garden. Long ago, I realised what kind of man you are, the love in your heart."

"I wasn't trying to buy you off, Father. I was able to purchase the engine and I wanted you to have it."

Father backed away and dropping into the chair clutching the tiny engine. He looked towards the ceiling to hide, I think, the tears in his eyes.

"It came from Germany, didn't it?"

"Yes, Father."

"And Captain von Holburg went out and purchased it for me, didn't he?"

"Does that make a difference?"

"I don't suppose it does, Devin," Father said, inspecting the engine even closer. "Terrible thing, this war."

"It is," I said.

"What do you lads think the German Catholics are praying for in their masses?"

"They must be praying for an end of the war."

"Aren't they praying for a German victory?"

"Well yes," Devin said slowly, "and people in Ireland are praying for an allied victory."

"Now, how does one sort these things out, Devin?"

My brother looked blankly at me and then Father. He believed that the priest was leading him on to some conclusion.

"I don't know," Devin answered cautiously.

"I don't either. I wonder if the Lord lets nationalism into his decisions. But, then, he could not condone a man like Hitler, could he?"

"I'm sure he does not," Devin answered quickly.

"These have been hard months for me. I've taken the children at the orphanage to my heart and when women come to me in the confessional and say, 'Bless me, Father, for I have sinned, I baked nine cakes for the German Navy' or 'I have knitted three sweaters for the wrong side', of course, I say 'Do you consider that a sin?' They only ask me and I have to tell them to be guided by their conscience."

Devin raced off his chair and came to his knees in front of Father Dunn.

"Is it a sin?" Devin asked, his hands shaking.

Father embraced him and said with an acute sense of pain, "It's very wrong what we are doing. But it cannot be a sin."

"Are you sure?" Devin said.

"Yes."

"We have no choice, Father. Did it ever strike you that

113

just as we were running into the worst of our financial troubles, the submarine should come into the harbour?"

"I have thought of it, Devin."

"And, perhaps, it was God who gave the man appendicitis so he had to be brought in here."

"Oh . . . it might be. God knows. I've prayed every night for guidance."

"Should we ask the Bishop over in Cork if we are doing the right thing?"

"No, no, Devin. We must not involve any more in this scheme. It is our doing and we will take the consequences on this earth or in heaven."

"And just what consequences do you see coming our way?"

"The Lord knows!"

This rather upset Devin. I believe that his conscience and emotions were in a worse state after having heard that Father Dunn was struggling with his own sense of morality. If someone in those days would have proclaimed the right or wrong of the matter, we would not have experienced the wrenching emotional wars that took place in each of us. I never realised that this moral struggle went through the whole of Dingle. And I suppose that each cake in an oven was, to some, a hand grenade thrown at a British soldier on the field of battle.

The morning following our meeting with Father Dunn, Devin sat down to type a letter. It was the first of such letters since he had sent his bill to Hitler. He typed this slowly and precisely as he did when he first wrote Henry Ford, Sr. I did not speak to Devin that morning or ask him to whom he was addressing the letter.

I might have guessed.

He showed me the correspondence at half-eleven and it was certainly the most profound of Devin's letter-writing career.

His Holiness
Pope Pius XII
The Vatican
Rome
Italy

114

My dear Pope,

You do not know me, but I am a Catholic business executive in the town of Dingle, County Kerry, Ireland.

Father Dunn, a very fine man, is our pastor here. Altogether, we have about fifteen hundred Catholics who are fine, upstanding people. The whole town, Father Dunn and myself have recently come to a moral crisis. So, I am writing to you in the hopes that your wisdom will prevail and tell us what to do. Father Dunn does not know of this letter and if you should meet him someday, I hope you will never tell him that I wrote to you.

Just at the beginning of the war, I evacuated some fifty sick orphans who were under the direction of my aunt, the Reverend Mother Mary Rose, from an old, inadequate building in the Lambeth district of London. Father, I do not believe that these little ones would have lived. In fact, the orphanage was bombed out in a future raid, and your local priest in the area, Father Smith, will corroborate my entire story. With the help of my brother, Billy, we brought the orphans to Dingle. Of course, the money ran out and we had no funds for medicine and other things that sick orphans need. Just then, a German submarine came into Dingle to let off a dying man. When the captain, a likable fellow named von Holburg, (also a Catholic), saw the food stuffs we had stored in our warehouse—I forgot to tell you that my brother and I are in the warehouse and haulage business—the captain wished to buy some of the things for the submarine service.

Naturally, we charged him a very high price and the profits went to support my aunt and the orphans.

The submarines are coming to Dingle at regular intervals and I can say that the entire town feels rather guilty, and we do not know if we should bear a guilt. We do not supply them with strategic goods such as petrol or ammunition, but even so, I know that Father Dunn is upset. He was over here at our house last night and I could tell the trouble that is on his mind. The question is obviously this:

115

No one likes to supply the wrong side. To us, the Germans represent the wrong side, the immoral side, because they started the war. And that is why the people of Dingle feel ashamed to be aiding them. But is it not the case that all war is wrong? Can there be a right or wrong to this thing? Perhaps, Father, you would be good enough to give us your wise counsel. The whole town is fighting with guilt.

If you decide that we are doing the wrong thing, I wonder if I could appeal to your charity and ask for a monthly donation for my aunt's orphans. They spend about two thousand pounds a month. The Bishop of Cork is sending about seventy pounds a month, so that would mean that our needs are in the area of nineteen hundred pounds each month.

Thank you, Father

> Yours in Christ,
> Devin H. C. Ryan, President
> Ryan Brothers International
> Dingle, County Kerry, Ireland
> Wilmington, Delaware, U.S.A.

TWENTY

About three days after Devin had written to the Pope, he came down to the breakfast table with a great grin on his face. It was that same kind of smile that always signalled an idea. (He took such pride in the authorship of his schemes.)

"Billy, while we are waiting to hear from the Pope, I think we will expand our trade with the Germans. We have something in Ireland that they need."

"And what is that?"

"Watchdogs."

"What was that again?" I asked quickly.

"We are a country of dogs. Now, obviously, the submarine base and other installations in occupied territory must be protected from the French Resistance. And all the concentration camps have dogs to keep the prisoners in. I've decided to have the nuns raise dogs for the Germans."

"Devin, that's going too far."

"But listen, we'll be pulling a trick on them. The Irish wolfhound is the largest dog in the world. He's as big as a small horse. Of course, he's stupid and wouldn't bite a soul. I'll get a wolfhound here and a cowardly German shepherd. We'll train the Irish wolfhound to attack the German shepherd. When Von Holburg sees this, he'll order thousands of wolfhound puppies."

"The German isn't that stupid," I said.

"We'll see. We'll see."

Of all the schemes developed by my brother this was the wildest. I figured that he had now lost his grip and that his mind was wandering too far from sanity. But once an idea came into Devin's head, it was never dropped. He had this desire to prove himself right. And it was not a day later that he went off in the Rolls returning late that night with two of the biggest dogs I had ever seen, one a German shepherd with cold dark eyes and the other a huge Irish wolfhound weighing some two hundred pounds. With Devin and the dogs came a Mr. Keen, a trainer and handler from Kilkenny. Two pens were built in the back of the house and for several days, Mr. Keen had the dogs performing all sorts of tricks. We heard barking and growling and when I asked Devin what was going on, he just simply looked at me and smiled.

"Ah, I can hardly wait for von Holburg to arrive," he said.

We knew that the Germans would come in sometime that week but the date was never certain. Finally, one morning about one o'clock, a quay watchman rang us up saying excitedly, "The fleet's here." We jumped up, dressed, and made several calls which awoke the whole town. Lights went on everywhere. Hundreds of women

117

with cakes and sweaters poured out of their little houses and rushed to the dock with the men. When we arrived, about two hundred Dingle people were standing out on the quay looking at the four black submarines tied abreast. Their deck guns were ready for fire since they interpreted the onrush of people to be hostile.

Captain von Holburg was standing on the dock when we arrived and he burst out, "What the hell are all these people doing here?"

"We had better go into the office quickly," Devin said, and we took the captain through the knot of people and retreated.

"What is all this?" von Holburg questioned.

"I've had troubles. The town found out about our trading and they organised a union to load our goods."

"Can we trust them?"

"No doubt about it," Devin said. "But I've had problems selling that champagne and perfume of yours. We're just not a nation of champagne drinkers and perfume wearers."

"You'll have to change, Devin, because I have seventy-five crates of champagne aboard."

"All right, then you'll have to take my sweaters and cakes. The women have banded together in a conspiracy. They're unionised! You'll have to help me out, too."

"I'll take the cakes and sweaters, and you unload the champagne."

"It all started with this Mrs. Rafferty and the green lantern signal," I said.

"Ah yes, the signal. We saw it through the periscope eight miles at sea. Very good idea."

"She discovered what we were doing and started this fuss."

"That's your problem. I warn you again—any disturbance which leads to interference here by the British will be dealt with in harsh terms."

"I understand," Devin sighed.

"We'd better unload, so my submarines can get to work on more important matters."

"When will you be back? We have over forty tons of food and other goods."

118

"Give us a month to finish our business on the Atlantic. Fifteen subs will be in. I've arranged the whole thing."

"Captain von Holburg, do I understand that you are using watchdogs in Germany?"

"Oh yes, we use good German shepherds around the camps and bases."

"We started using German shepherds around here, too."

"What for, Devin?"

"We wanted to protect your goods in the warehouse."

"Very clever of you."

"But we've had trouble with German shepherd dogs."

"How could you? They're the best attackers in the world."

"I'm afraid they are basically cowards. We've had five of them, and we had to give them away in favour of our own Irish wolfhound."

"That cannot be. The German shepherd is the toughest dog in the world. I've had two of them myself—wonderful, faithful dogs. There is no equal to them."

"Except for the Irish wolfhound," Devin said smartly.

"The shepherd could take the Irish wolfhound any day."

"Would you bet on that?"

"Of course I would," the German said resolutely and laughed.

On that remark, Devin showed the captain around to the side of our warehouse. And there chained to the side was the growling, fanged German shepherd. He looked at us and rumbled, letting his teeth flash in the night lights.

"Don't get too close; he's dangerous," Devin said.

"Then, you agree he's vicious, Devin?" von Holburg said.

Devin unchained the dog and he still continued to snarl. We walked to the other side of the warehouse and in the shadows, I saw Mr. Keen standing as if pretending to be out for an evening cigarette. He winked at Devin and then nodded.

"What the hell is that!" von Holburg cried as the gigantic Irish wolfhound with his huge, slobbering mouth hanging open leaped forth.

119

"That, captain, is the most vicious dog in the world."

The captain shrank back as the huge animal stood up on his hind legs letting out a growl. Suddenly, we noticed the German shepherd. His tail was between his legs. Devin let the wolfhound off his chain and the animal pounced upon the shepherd even before it could dash away. The Irish dog opened his mouth and took the entire neck of the shepherd within his jaws. There was a horrible sound; it was a battle to the death.

"Fight! Fight!" Captain von Holburg said to the German dog.

"He's just no match for the Irish dog."

The two animals rolled over and over in the darkness, and finally the wolfhound dragged the shepherd over by the collar, and again Devin looked towards Mr. Keen with a smile on his face.

"Do you believe me now?" Devin asked.

"I have never seen such a wild animal," the German said.

We retired to the office as both dogs started barking and Devin said, "Captain, we can make thousands of pounds with these dogs."

"By taking them back to Germany?"

"Yes, you could use these hounds as watchdogs."

"But they might bite my men and we could not load too many on the submarine."

"What about puppies? They could be trained by your own forces."

"Very interesting proposal, Devin. Very interesting. All right, how much?"

"Ten pounds an animal. They're worth twice as much."

"We'll take seventy-five on the next trip in, but I say to you—if they do not work out, you must give us a credit."

"Of course; everything we sell is on approval. That is the only way the Ryan Brothers International work. A money-back guarantee."

We negotiated the payments and went to the quay. By that time, the women were serving the submarine crews coffee and cake, and bottles of Irish whiskey were being passed around. Fifty boxes of homemade jellies and vegetable tins were loaded and the dock was soon piled high with champagne crates, enough to wash out every mouth in Ireland. Our dock labourers, half of them drunk, stumbled over the submarines with the cases. Big Tim, hauling more than his share of champagne, fell into the harbour between two subs. The German sailors tried on their Irish sweaters and as the hours passed, it was impossible to tell who was German and who was Irish. The blending was quite remarkable.

An hour before dawn, the subs started their Diesels and, one by one, they threw off their dock lines and disappeared into the darkness. The women cheered and the men sang songs of Ireland.

When the submarines had slipped away. Mr. Keen came out to the end of the quay holding both the dogs who were now wagging their tails and kissing each other with great sweeps of their wet tongues.

"How was that now, Mr. Ryan?"

"Beautiful. What a show. The Germans believed the whole thing."

"How did you prod them into a fight, Mr. Keen?" I asked.

"Just trained them to play hard."

"They were just playing?"

"But with much noise."

"Mr. Keen, I hope we can get hold of seventy-five wolfhound puppies."

"We'll do it, Mr. Ryan."

I had not the slightest doubt in my mind that every dog in Ireland would soon be in Dingle. That, too, gave rise to new frights.

TWENTY-ONE

It was to be the best Christmas in the history of Dingle. New wealth was about, and all the champagne that we could not sell went into a general fund at the "Bee". It was sold for three shillings a bottle. So, the townsmen found a new taste and the word changed from, "Have a pint with me" to "Have a little champagne with me". Even Mrs. Rafferty took to drinking the elixir and we worried over this because her failure to perform her duty might well bring us to the most embarrassing end. Even though everyone in the town suffered from a continual hangover, there was joy all about. People talked to each other, smiled where before they grumbled; and I suppose it was the presence of the nuns and the orphans which gave us the most happiness.

Somehow in those weeks we forgot from where the wealth originated; we merely lived on as if a new society had been born into this small corner of Ireland. Devin was the most joyous of all. He repeated the story of the dogs and Mr. Keen's trick to everyone in Dingle, and they hailed my brother as some new, exalted hero. (Everyone was secretly delighted that something had been put over on the shrewd Germans.) It was the fortnight of Christmas that Devin announced to Mr. Keen and myself that we were going up to Dublin for Christmas presents. It was also to be a dog-buying trip. Again, Devin thought the project out and came up with a rather clever way to fetch seventy-five hounds back to Dingle.

"I am putting our famous bus back into service. Now, it'll be an animal van."

In my mind I could just see seventy-five howling

wolfhounds fighting and scrambling in the double-decker bus and, in one sweep, all of them rushing downstairs to devour us as a punishment for our deeds. At any rate, we packed our best suits and motored to the orphanage. We were going to tell the Reverend Mother that hundreds of little dogs were coming to stay with us for a time, and as Devin so nicely put it to our aunt,

"You see, Reverend Mother, the puppies are orphan puppies. And the children will enjoy the little orphan animals."

The woman was quite willing to go along with anything that Devin suggested because in her mind he was a saviour. While we were telling the Reverend Mother about our trip to Dublin, she suddenly interrupted,

"Have you met our new physiotherapist, direct from Dublin?"

"No, I haven't," Devin said.

Mother Superior showed them into another room and in walked the most sultry, spidery, ginger-haired, sexy-looking physiotherapist in all the world. She appeared to be a cross between a secret agent and a society girl. She had a dark tan, long flowing hair which she brushed back with flicks of her shoulder, and her breasts were elegantly packed into her tight white uniform.

"Oh my dear Kate, I do want you to meet my nephews, Devin Ryan and his brother, Billy Ryan. This is Kate Gowan."

"Mr. Ryan," she said in a deep voice as she flowed across the room holding out her hand for us to shake.

Devin and I came to our feet in a fraction of a second.

"Hello," Devin said, "and how are you enjoying working with my aunt, I mean, the Reverend Mother?" There was a fluster in his voice, the first that I could remember.

"There is so much to be done, isn't there, Mr. Ryan?"

"Yes, yes. Well, ah . . . . call me Devin."

"I've heard *everything* about you."

"Don't believe what you hear," Devin said, half-laughing.

"I want to believe everything," she said in a soft tone which was mellowed by her deep, seductive look.

"Well . . . .", Devin staggered.

123

"I want you to tell me everything," she said commandingly.

" . . . I mean . . . about what?"

"Your life, how you came to know the world leaders, your influential friends who come to call."

"What have you heard about my . . ah . . influential friends?"

"I want you to tell me . . . . everything," she repeated in a rumbling, seductive voice.

Devin was swept off his feet and he fell deeply, madly in love that afternoon at the orphanage. The Reverend Mother smiled and she knew that in some small way she had paid Devin back for all his generosity.

Ronnie drove Devin in the Rolls and just before we started from the orphanage, Devin leaned from the rear window of the motor car and grasped Kate's hand. I heard him say, "I shall be thinking about you."

They smiled at each other endlessly as she walked along with the Rolls waving to Devin, the grey of her eyes catching the morning sunlight. Kate did not notice Mr. Keen and myself as we passed driving the double-decker bus. I felt, then, that the missing link in the life of Devin Ryan had just dropped into place.

Up through Clare and Galway we stopped at farm after farm, and our dog-buying mission seemed to be more successful than anyone had realised it would be. Every poor puppy in the land was placed upstairs in the bus which had been prepared with old burlap sacks. Most of the dogs seemed strange to me and I was not sure that we were purchasing wolfhounds. They were all full of fight and they barked endlessly and soon the bus was a stenching, echoing hell on wheels.

"Don't give up, Billy," Devin would say as he leaned out of the Rolls showing me his new love-filled eyes.

"Why don't you drive this thing, Devin?"

"It's my blood pressure again, Billy. Believe me, I can feel the pressure going up and up."

By the time we reached County Wicklow, there were over sixty yelping puppies on both levels of the bus. Mr. Keen was drinking heavily as he separated them. Every now and then I would find a dog in my lap or one sinking his needle-like baby teeth into my ankles. We reached Dublin on a cold afternoon and drew up to the Brazen Head pub for a bit of warmth. When we opened the door, all the puppies ran out and we had to chase them halfway down the hill to the River Liffey.

That night we registered at the Shelbourne Hotel and Mr. Keen reminded Devin that the dogs could not stay out in the bus overnight. And so we began to smuggle them upstairs under our coats, but we had only managed to land four or five in our rooms when the general manager hurried in.

"You can't bring all those dogs up here! They're barking and the Garda is ready to haul the bus away!"

We rushed downstairs and on the side street seven or eight police were standing around the bus looking in with their torches.

"Would you come along to the police station, Mr. Ryan?" the officer said pleasantly.

We were taken into a small room and one of the inspectors began asking some routine questions which raised the fright in our hearts.

"Where did you come by that bus, Mr. Ryan?"

"In England," Devin answered.

"Do you collect busses?"

"We brought little orphans over in it so they could escape the blitz. They're in Dingle now."

"And what are you planning to do with the dogs?"

"They're Christmas presents for the orphans."

"You mean each orphan will receive a present of a dog?"

"Yes."

That sounded too preposterous even for a Devin Ryan story, and the inspector rang through to the Reverend Mother asking her to corroborate the tale. We only heard bits of the conversation, but the inspector did say,

"You mean, Reverend Mother, that there will be seventy-five wolfhounds at your orphanage? I see . . . . I see. . . . Well, I suppose the children will like . . . . but seventy-five. Oh yes, you can understand our concern finding a double-decker bus outside the Shelbourne Hotel loaded with seventy-five puppies. Rather unusual, I would say."

A heated garage was found for the bus and Mr. Keen, armed with some support from his bottle of Jameson, spent the night taking care of the dogs.

Not a puppy died on the way down to Dingle despite the bitter rain-swept weather, but I had nine puppy bites and the worst cold I can remember. Devin merely seemed aloof; he sat in the back of the Rolls with presents for the nuns and a stack of brightly wrapped boxes with big bows on their way to Kate.

During the week of our return, we built running pens for the puppies and kept them in the bus which they had grown to like. We heated the vehicle with a warm air duct taken off the central heating system at the orphanage. Of course, some of the dogs were let into the orphanage, and Mother Mary Rose said that a few of the children who had never moved certain muscles were now exercising them as they chased the animals about the place. Even Kate told Devin that he had out-performed the best therapist in the world.

"But happiness is the best therapy," Devin said.

Christmas Eve a huge fire was built in the main room of the orphanage and the whole town came to bring their presents to the children and the nuns. There was great happiness and we all sang hymns led by Father Dunn and my aunt. Each of the dogs was allowed inside that evening and with the children holding them, the Reverend Mother stood up and presented Devin with a present from the nuns. It was a fine edition of Saint Thomas and a small speech went along with it.

"We all know what Devin has done for the nuns and the children. Through his world-wide business connections, he has taken up the needs of this poor orphanage and collected funds from his generous friends. We could only afford this small present, but with it go our prayers and good hopes for the continued success of Devin Ryan."

Kate grasped Devin's hand and he looked to the floor and his eyes did not meet Father Dunn's. This was the worst emotional upheaval within the two of them yet, and my own emotions were strangely mixed on that Christmas Eve.

The evening was one I shall never forget. The nuns had

cooked five Christmas geese for us and the feast was enjoyed by all. During each course, Devin and Father Dunn were taking hot toddies prepared by Kate. At the end of the meal, Devin was well in his cups in a sweet, glowing way. (Indeed, I had never seen him quite like this in my life. It was partly the Jameson's, partly love, and partly the fact that he wished to crowd from his mind the unthinkable.) Finally, after Reverend Mother's sherry trifle, Devin rose to his feet and said to all gathered,

"Now to complete this great and wonderful feast, I will read, with everyone's permission, my favorite Christmas story. To me, this story says everything about Christmas except for the gospels of that night," Devin bowed his head in apology to Father Dunn at that point. "In my own words, Charles Dickens's *A Christmas Carol.*"

We gathered around—Father Dunn, the seventy-five whimpering dogs, the nuns, Dr. Hawkins, Mother Mary Rose, Kate, the orphans and myself. Devin stood, wobbly as he was, and opened a beautifully bound copy of *A Christmas Carol* from Uncle Shemas's old collection:

"Morley was dead . . . . dead as a doornail . . ." Devin began with a deep rasp in his voice.

On the first line I happened to be looking towards the children and I saw gleam come into their eyes; I must say that no one could have read that brilliant story with more compassion, feeling, love and understanding than Devin Ryan. He acted out each character: Scrooge with his hard, griping voice; Tiny Tim in his halting way; and Bob Cratchit in his tone of understanding.

It went on for slightly over two hours. There was not one dry eye in the orphanage. The idea of Christmas had been brought to Dingle.

But it was not the *only* idea of that night.

After the reading and the "Good Nights" and "Merry Christmases", I went along to check the warehouse. By the front door, there was a pile of small, crudely wrapped packages. I opened the letter on top because it was addressed to both of us.

These are for the nuns, the children and my friends, the Ryan brothers. I looked in on the way into St.

Nazaire as my commanding officer promised me that the submarine would be in from the Atlantic on Christmas Eve. You see, we also celebrate Christmas in Germany and I give you these presents because they are more than ever symbolic this year. I cannot help but think of the first Christmas and what it meant.

Best wishes for a profitable New Year.

Your friend,
Hans von Holburg

TWENTY-TWO

It was the worst January in the history of Dingle. One night when the snow was falling—something quite unusual for the southern coast of Ireland—eleven German submarines put into our quay. It was the biggest transfer yet, and Father Dunn came down to see it. At the end of loading, some ninety sweaters, two hundred and four cakes, seventy-one pies, seven tons of food goods and fifty puppies had been put into the submarines.

Our great concern that night was keeping the secret from the nuns. This we did, and that was all that mattered.

One fine Sunday in early March, Devin took us in the Rolls for a picnic at a certain strand near Ballyferriter, the last town on the peninsula. He kindly invited Father Dunn to join us also. Mrs. O'Connor prepared a true gourmet lunch. (Some things were back to normal.) I remember she packed grouse and pheasant sandwiches along with champagne, wine and little cakes rolled and baked over delicate slices of good lean bacon. The day was warm and the sun blessed us with hardly a cloud in the sky. Father Dunn sat in the back of the car enjoying the breeze and

Kate was beside him, sultry as usual. As the car twisted and turned along the road by the sea, Devin went on to explain his hopes for this barren land. Someplace along the way, he decided that the area should be turned into an industrial site because of our deepwater harbour, and his thoughts flew aloft that afternoon. He envisioned a huge power plant, a motor car factory, and the whole countryside turned into some kind of economic paradise with himself at the controls. Devin was no more truly interested in factories than he was in celery production, but he saw wealth in manufacturing and the true merchant in him came out in wild flights of his energetic fancy.

We arrived at the spot picked out by my brother. The tall lush grass waved to the border of the sea; this gave way to short, rock-filled cliffs which somehow kept back the invasion of winter gales. On one side the cliffs fell into the land to form a miniature harbour; at the end of this was the brightest, cleanest sand in the world. Devin called it a magic strand. And it was. Tucked into the rich green hills, this small patch of virgin sand had never been ruined by chocolate-papers or empty tins. This little spot was unknown to everyone except the few farmers who walked along this way on their journey home.

We picked out the softest spot in the grass overlooking the strand. The colours, I remember, were untainted by the haze of rain-spent clouds. There was a purity here, a freshness given by the raw clarity of sky and earth. Each one of us felt good and close to the beautiful land of Dingle. (In moments like these, we saw the richness of our place and we appreciated the spot God had given us. It was truly a blessing when the rain did not hide what the land wanted to show us.) Well, we took out our wool blankets and spread them across the meadow. The champagne was cool in an elegant silver ice bucket purchased when Devin was going through his most avid gourmet and good-living period. We drank for a time and told stories we remembered from childhood when we sat before the peat fire and listened to the elders swap folklore. (How sad it is that these traditions are not carried on today. Our imaginations were bubbled by these rich fables; in the case of Devin Ryan, he never forgot the myths of his early childhood. He carried these to his adult years and who could say it hurt him the slightest?) The air remained clean and good as each tongue was loosened with the spirits.

Somehow my eye happened to catch sight of something on the gentle waves moving towards the strand. A fright gripped me and I suggested that we should pack up and leave.

"Leave? Why should we leave?" Devin said, leaning back to find a place in Kate's lap.

Father Dunn was relaxing on one elbow so that he could not see the water washing the strand.

"How about taking a walk with me, Father Dunn. Yes, we could go up and see this beautiful spot from the hill."

"Thank you, Billy, but my legs aren't what they used to be with this constant dampness."

"Are you sure?" I asked.

"No, thank you."

"Don't bother Father Dunn. He's enjoying himself as he is," Devin added.

I knew there was nothing I could do. Out of the corner of my eye I saw the sight slowly drifting towards us. God, how I prayed in those moments for this thing to go away or slip beneath the waves.

The battered lifeboat would not disappear. I bit into the flesh of my tongue as it got closer, for hanging lifelessly over the side of the rail, dangling like a wet stuffed doll, was a human arm. I edged between Father Dunn and the sight; in case he sat straight, he would not see this horror coming towards us. Hail Marys bounced around in my heart and as they reached my throat I seemed to swallow them. Sweat came under my arms and along my forehead, too.

"Let's all take a nice walk to digest our meal," I suggested.

"Meals are digested by rest. In that way," Devin said, "the stomach juices can go about their work undisturbed."

"But shouldn't we get some exercise? You know—walk and smell the air, breathe the sweet scent of flowers into our lungs?"

"Billy, will you sit and relax. Devin is a tired

businessman. He needs this rest. Don't you, Devin?" Kate said.

"Indeed I do. It's the first rest I've had in a fortnight or even longer."

I half turned my head and peered towards the water. The lifeboat was getting closer now. It would only be a few seconds before they saw it. Somehow they reclined further back and the minutes went on endlessly as the boat beached on the strand and turned sideways. The arm of the lone survivor grew into the dreadful sight of a limp, waterlogged corpse, wrinkled and grey-green. My heart sent up more prayers and I do not remember now if I was praying for the man's soul or for him and his boat to go away. Kate rose to stretch herself and she made the first frightful yell.

"Look, there's a man in a boat!"

"Tell him to go away and leave us in peace," Devin said.

"Well now, Devin, I don't think he's about to go away of his own power. He looks rather dead," she said.

Up popped Father Dunn and Devin, and I turned as if to discover this horror for the first time. We ran to the edge of the strand and Father Dunn approached first.

The man was cold dead.

Father Dunn made sure of that and we stood back as he gave the last rites. Only the sounds of Father Dunn's Latin mixed with the gently breaking surf could be heard. He finally came to the end of the prayer and each of us murmured, "Amen". Then, there followed an ungodly silence as we stared towards the dead sailor. We stood there locked in awe for long minutes until Father Dunn spoke.

"The man, God rest his soul, should get a decent burial. I'll say a high mass for him. This is a dreadful way to go. He must have had a home somewhere and a family to love him. He'll never come back to his home now."

Father's words were touching because Kate started to cry and I caught a lump in my throat. Devin peered at the sand under his feet and I know he was steeped in sorrow.

"All right now," Devin said finally in a straight, direct voice, "don't think it's our fault. That's what is in your mind and I know it. Hundreds of sailors are killed every day. If a torpedo doesn't get them, storms will. We're not the murderers so let's keep our wits about us."

But Father Dunn merely continued to stare at Devin. My brother was not one to be stared down or shamed by looks. He walked right up to the lifeboat saying, "I'll take care of the man."

Devin slid his arms around the sailor's chest and with a heave, he landed the corpse on the beach before us.

"Oh, God!" Kate said, seeing the man's grey-green skin glistening between the water wrinkles. Father Dunn made the sign of the cross once again; and not until then, did we notice the faint markings on the breast of the life jacket.

"The Maltese cross," Devin shouted. "Why, it's the Maltese cross!"

(We found out sometime after Father Dunn had said a mass and we had put the German beneath the sod near the little church in Dunquin, that Ludwig Heller was a torpedo man aboard a German submarine. His craft was forced to the surface by an Allied destroyer. And as it happened, he dived over the side and found a deserted lifeboat from a perished cargo steamer. Even now, so many years later, my thoughts often flash back to that sunny day on the strand. The picture of the dead sailor washing ashore often reaches across my mind. I don't think any other impression has moved me quite so much or demonstrated so vividly the complete folly of this idiotic adventure called war.)

TWENTY-THREE

The first warm weather came to Dingle during the following weeks. The time was getting close for another U-boat visit; our warehouse was filled to both doors, and each night we posted a watch by the harbour mouth, who would warn us ahead if the submarines slid past. From his watch position, he could look up towards the headland and see if Mrs. Rafferty kept the signal light going all night. I was frankly worried over this woman. Devin had given her a full case of champagne, and I saw her weaving about the town several days in a row always carrying a half-eaten cake. Perhaps she needed an assistant lightkeeper, but we did not wish to begin a labour precedent by attaching assistants to every job; we were already burdened by too many helpers.

We had just come back from the warehouse when our lookout signalled with his torch. The light was picked up by the man on the quay who rang us. We made but one phone call and immediately a chain reaction began. The "Bee" emptied, mixing bowls and knitting needles were put aside; doors opened and soon there could be heard that little rattle of anxious feet moving over the Dingle cobbles towards our quay.

We jumped into the motor car yelling back that Mrs. O'Connor should prepare for a feast. Devin was planning a night of entertainment which was very much a part of international trade. Kate stayed behind to assist Mrs. O'Connor and I knew then that this would not be an easy evening. We drove out along the harbour mouth road. The afterglow still remained and, obviously, the submarines had lingered under the water until the light over the mountain disappeared. When they spied the green signal on Dunmore Head, they started through the harbour opening. There was just enough brightness from a low moon to see these shapes moving in like a steady, slithering line of black water rats. It was an ominous scene, somewhat horrifying, and I felt the old flutter again.

"We better be getting down there," Devin said. He pressed the motor car into gear and we roared off towards the quay. A thick crowd, the whole town to be more accurate, was milling around the wire gates. Devin drove his car through, blowing the hooter and waving to the happy women who were holding heaps of sweaters and cake boxes.

"Get back there. We'll open the gates just as soon as I make positive identification."

We drove to the very end of the stone dock just as the first submarine was tossing its lines over. Devin got out and stood watching his men, half drunk as they were, trying to fit the hemp around our mooring bits. There were shouts and counter shouts in German. One by one they came, nine in all, and finally Hans stepped onto the quay, more worn and exhausted than we had ever seen him. Even in the dim lights, his face seemed to have aged a hundred years. The submarines behind him were streaked with rust and that same fetid odour was upon the docks in a matter of minutes as if the tops of tins containing rotten food had suddenly been pried open.

"Captain, good to see you. Welcome to Dingle once more," Devin said, extending his hand.

"Good evening."

"How is the war going?"

"The war, ah . . . . it is getting to be dangerous work," the German said. "You should be quite happy with your safety, Devin."

"Who is safe in this world today?"

"I'm too tired to answer that one. Now, is everything ready?"

"The very best—beautiful hams, beef sides, American cigarettes, silk stockings of the highest quality."

"Good. Good. There hasn't been any dissension in this town of yours, has there?"

"Of course not. I merely told them you would blow up the place if someone talked."

The German laughed, but even in his amusement there was a dead serious look about him.

"Now, captain, I want you to forget the war, the unpleasantness of it all. We're preparing a party in your honour, a fine dinner with whiskey and wine, the delicate cooking of Mrs. O'Connor. I extend the invitation to all your commanders. We'll eat, drink and have a short discussion about the accounts. While we're busy, my men can assist yours in loading the submarines."

"I accept your hospitality, Devin. But, I warn you, we might become loud and uncontrollable."

"Anything's all right. I'm only sorry we cannot offer you female companionship, but you know the difficulty with that sort of thing in Ireland."

"We're all happily married men. Don't worry about it."

Shortly after, we met all of the captains—an intelligent,

English-speaking group of men. A bottle of Irish whiskey was passed around. The dock came alive with the chatter of German sailors in Irish sweaters, drinking coffee and whiskey and pushing huge mounds of cake into their mouths. The rest of that night is only a blur now.

Somehow just before dawn, the submarines were loaded and the accounts settled. Two of the German sailors decided that this landfall was better than serving the German cause under the Atlantic. They failed to return to their ship and a search did not uncover them.

Diesels kicked over and the line of fully loaded subs left Dingle harbour. Devin and I were barely sober as we motored to the head of the harbour and watched the disappearing wolf pack. The light was spreading swiftly across the water now and the submarine captains, as drunk as they were, realised they had waited too long. The second they reached the open water, their bows started down.

"God damn it," Devin screamed out, "get the hell out of there!"

He stood up in the motor car covering his face. The last submarine moved under to the side of the others. The captain probably had trouble seeing the blur of subs in front of him and he dove his boat right into a thick web of fishing nets. Stakes holding the nets popped under the pressure like toothpicks bitten off by a giant fish. The submarine was just under, going along slowly at periscope depth (whatever depth that is), and then suddenly the oily, black water turned into a foaming, white whirlpool.

"He's done it!" Devin yelled.

"Do you think he's caught?"

"He cut through the nets all right, but his props are tangled."

Soon the wash from the motors stopped, bearing out Devin's theory. The surface went dark again and then little bubbles caught the morning light. He was blowing his tanks. Just the top of the conning tower appeared above the surface like the tooth of a sea creature airing in the morning light. Several men came from the conning tower with tools in their hands and wearing some sort of underwater breathing device. They dived overboard with the idea of cutting away the rope.

"They won't do it," Devin said. "The net is too fine. It's ground into the shaft."

We drove at a full seventy miles an hour around the harbour road back onto the quay. (Devin, I must admit, handled this one with dispatch and creative judgment.) He jumped out and slapped two mackerel fishermen on the face.

"Get up! We've got troubles."

The men came to light; Devin got them to start their beam trawler without quite understanding what it was all about. My brother stopped in his tracks and his face had the excited flush of deep thought.

"Follow me, every one of you."

We ran behind him back towards the warehouse. He burst inside the door and found six of our union dockers sprawled in sleep on the gold carpet.

"Up! Up! There's a disaster. A sub's in trouble just outside the harbour. Get all the canvas covers from the vans and the warehouse. Hurry up or there'll be hell fire around here! Come with me, Billy."

We raced across from the warehouse into the marine shipyard of Tumulty & Son. Although we were harbour neighbours, Tumulty never so much as greeted us. He was a stern man who always walked around with a "bosun's knife" hanging from his rotund midsection. There was something threatening about him; it could have been his silence. At any rate, we tore into his office and Devin shouted out before the man even lifted his head from his cup of morning tea.

"Tumulty, one of our subs is in trouble. I want every canvas duck cover you have in this place, about ten planks and your work boats."

Old Tumulty just sat there and looked at Devin with his whiskered chin hanging slack.

"Be quick about you," Devin demanded.

"So, you're in trouble, is that it? Well, you can't have me men and boats. We've got work here."

"You'll have British bombs. A sub is caught in the nets. She's out there plain as day, so you better be working for us before the British patrol planes spot her and drop bombs all about here. Now, get yourself up before it's too late."

Devin gave the huge, round man a slight push. And he reacted, I suppose, out of some kind of instant fright—the thought of black specks in the sky dropping bombs on his yard.

Five boats, three beam trawlers and two work craft from the yard reached the submarine. The captain, a Walter Bonmer who had got very drunk the night before, stood on the lip of the conning tower, white and drawn.

"You should have cleared these nets, Herr Ryan." He was very sober by this time.

"And you should have followed the other boats."

"We did. We did," he called.

"But they didn't hit the nets."

The captain just shook his head.

"We have to act fast," Devin said. "The outline of your boat can be seen from the air."

"Blow all your tanks; we're about to cover you with canvas tarpaulins. We'll tow you in and have the Tumulty Shipyard clear your props."

"That's too dangerous, Herr Ryan."

"You'll never free yourself."

There was a short period of looking and thinking. We bobbed in silence, our work boats standing off the submarine about ten yards. Somewhere, a high pitched buzz filled the quiet morning; it became louder and we looked up through hazy, broken clouds. Devin jumped to the wheel of Tumulty's work boat; he shoved open the throttle; the engine roared.

"Follow me!" he screamed to the beam trawlers.

Devin manoeuvred the boat across the submerged foresection of the sub. He ordered the other boats to take up positions towards the stern section. While this was going on, a formation of British planes broke through the clouds; they looked like a bunch of black wasps going about their business. The sub captain glanced up so alarmed he could neither speak nor gasp.

"Throw your clutches in neutral. Run the hell out of the engines," Devin yelled.

It then occurred to me what he was doing. The five

work vessels hugged the submarine, their props spitting out a shower of white foam which danced about the surface. A full minute seemed to pass as we looked into the sky to see the black wings fade off into the morning light.

Devin fell back against the bulwark of the work boat sighing with relief. He had saved the U-boat and averted an international incident, I am sure. By hugging the boats close to the sub and breaking the surface with wash, he thus destroyed that revealing underwater silhouette which would have inspired a few well-placed explosives.

"All right now, captain, I am in charge," Devin said without the slightest hesitation in his voice.

The German turned his pasty face and nodded unconditional agreement. That settled, Devin went on.

"Bring your sub to the surface."

The German yelled something down the conning tower hatch and we cleared the submarine as she blew her tanks and fully surfaced. Then Devin ordered the work boats alongside. He began placing planks across the decks in a tangent fashion. These were covered with tarpaulins; the sub again lost its silhouette and we began to tow the hidden warship into Dingle harbour.

The town was still sleeping, drunk from the night before, and no one rushed to the quay to witness this strange covered hull being pushed, stern first, into the Tumulty yard. Devin again demonstrated the resources of his young mind. The stern section was tied to the marine slip-way, the forward part submerged just under the surface. The hauling winches whirled and the slip-way tugged at the heaviest load in its life. There were yells and commands from Devin; the German crew appeared on deck rather confused by the whole operation. Finally, the top blades of the props broke water just as the winch belched and then exploded, sending a fine white smoke trailing in the air.

"You'll pay for this, Ryan!" Tumulty screamed.

Devin did not mind, but merely ordered the work boats over the submerged area of the sub. It was a laughable sight—everyone yelling and panting and the sub sticking its tail from the water like a desperately ill walrus. At least she was covered from the air. When Tumulty cooled down, his men started to work on the props, a tangled, engaged glob of black cord. Devin and I were standing beside the stern section and the German sailors were sauntering about with their hands in their pockets. It was not clear who was Irish and who was German because the crew were wearing thick knitted sweaters and most of them meandered back and forth just gawking.

I happened to turn about and my eye wandered towards the roadway, the space between our warehouse and Tumulty's. Several elderly women were sitting there on the tiny stools with canvas painting boards fixed on portable easels.

"Oh God," I thought to myself.

I nudged Devin to slide his eyes that way. He brought his hands over his face and began to think. In a split second, he marched up to the roadway signalling me to follow. They had just started to sketch the scene and a lady in an absurdly flowered hat was their art mistress, I suppose, because she strolled around making poetic statements about the clear morning colours. From that position, no one could really tell what the black hulk coming from the water represented. Some of them had drawn in the shape and Devin moved right up to the instructor.

"Good morning, ladies. Good morning. Welcome to Dingle."

"Thank you," said the instructor. "We're from the Killarney painting classes. Our annual outing, you know."

"I'm Devin Ryan, president of that warehouse company and a great art lover. But, ladies, I must warn you," Devin went on in a whispering tone, "there's no sense in painting this scene."

"We thought it was charming."

"Oh, it is. Make no mistake about that. But you see, we'll be moving all the boats in an hour. Appreciating art as I do, I certainly don't want you to waste your time and have the subject move. May I suggest another subject? How would you like my vice-president, Mr. Billy Ryan, to take you ladies to the most beautiful spot in Ireland. Not too far from here. It's ringed with colour and shapes that you could capture with your obvious talent."

"That would be splendid."

"I'll have Mr. Billy Ryan personally take you in our slightly war-damaged Rolls to Dunquin. That's where the road curves and off in the distance are the famous Blasket Islands in all their morning colours."

"What do you think, girls? Mr. Ryan has made a generous offer."

They packed up and I drove the ladies out to the Dunquin headlands where they set up their easels once again. Promising to pick them up later, I motored back into Dingle.

They had cleared one prop of the mesh and the other one was almost untangled. Just after eleven, we rigged the canvas over the sub and towed her to the outer harbour. The skipper clasped Devin's hand, tried his engine shafts and with the canvas still on top, submerged leaving only bubbles and canvas on the surface. We looked after the bubbles for a time and Devin stroked his angular chin.

(Ah, one more, Devin Ryan.)

TWENTY-FOUR

Spring came early that year and Devin was in love. My brother stopped caring about our submarine trade. He was writing daily love letters to Kate at the orphanage. In the late afternoons when she had finished her work, I would see them walking on the grassy hills around Dingle holding hands and exchanging small kisses. Our export programme with the Germans had taken on a massive escalation. We were holding orders for over ninety tons of food and I was quite certain that this might arouse suspicion. With Devin dreamily walking around the office humming to himself, it was most difficult to reach him and decide on a security programme, or at least some way politely to level off the volume of business. (Father Dunn told us

140

that the frequency of women confessing to their "cake baking" for the Germans was directly proportional to the tonnage we were loading.)

One week in early May, Father Dunn dropped in and I knew immediately that it was not to be a pleasant visit. Kate was eating with us that evening and we asked the priest if he would not care to take his meal at our table.

"That's nice of you," Father said. "Yes, I will sit with you."

He sat down and Kate smiled at him and she moved her hand into Devin's. (Kate was our spy at the orphanage and she reported all the doings of the nuns. We were particularly anxious that no news or information reach the Reverend Mother or the children.)

"Devin, I've been thinking about the dogs."

"What about them, Father?"

"I cannot in good conscience say that those hounds are non-strategic."

"Well, Father, I don't think they're weapons of war."

"And besides, the children love the dogs at the orphanage," Kate added.

"But what do the nuns say when suddenly the dogs disappear one night?" Father asked.

"I simply tell the Reverend Mother that they are going for advanced training. And, of course, we do replace them with new puppies."

"It's a dangerous thing, Devin," Father sighed. "The women still come to me confessing that they are baking cakes for Hitler."

"Well, it makes them feel better I'm certain."

"But this thing has turned the town into a moral shambles. Peaceful men and women are drinking too much. All they can think of is making more and more money from the Germans. What I fear, Devin, is that we might not be able to halt this thing even when we have enough to run the orphanage."

All through Father's conversation Devin was looking at Kate and I do not believe he heard one word of what was said, nor did he care. But Father was beginning to become demented by the pressure forced upon him in his confessional. All that spring he did not amuse himself with his

141

trains nor ride around on his bike as was his habit in fair weather. Father Dunn's conflicts with himself were made more acute even as he sat at our table that evening. Mrs. O'Connor announced that Mrs. Rafferty was at the door with a delegation of ladies from the town.

"Oh no!" Devin yelled. "Please, no Mrs. Rafferty, not tonight!"

"I heard that, Devin Ryan," she said, moving slowly into the room. When she saw Father Dunn, she smiled. A new calmness had come into her voice.

"Now, Mr. Ryan and Father Dunn, we've just had a meeting . . . ."

"We simply can't use more pies or sweaters or bread. The Germans just won't take them," Devin interrupted.

"It's not that. We had a meeting and decided that we were going to give all our profits to the orphanage and the men are going to put in their money, too."

Mrs. Rafferty handed Devin a bank-order for over seven hundred pounds.

"This is very generous of you, Mrs. Rafferty, I'm sure," Devin said heartfully.

(The fact that the whole of Dingle had given their profits to the orphanage was interpreted by Father Dunn to mean that there was some guilt about, and this made the priest's task even more difficult. I personally felt that Mrs. Rafferty was only expressing the generosity of those in Dingle, and it was not the softening of a moral problem.)

Devin said a few words of appreciation to the delegation and returned to the table and opened a bottle of champagne. He was looking at Kate warmly and with a certain gulp to his voice, he said,

"We might as well make the announcement now as long as Father is present. Kate and I have decided to get married and we would like you to marry us in Dingle, Father, at a very high evening mass."

"Congratulations, Devin," Father said.

Mrs. O'Connor who was standing near burst into tears and kissed Devin. "Oh, I think it is wonderful," she sobbed.

For the next three weeks Devin was even more dazed. He hardly put his mind to the task of running our business. His dream might have lasted forever if it had not been for Kate's discovery in the morning Dublin paper. She rushed into our office carrying a stack of papers which she had collected at the orphanage.

"Devin, look at this."

"What, darling," he said smiling affectionately.

Kate handed me a copy and my heart pounded quickly against my chest. The words blared out at us like painful stabs. Black headlines on the *Dublin Independent* announced:

IRELAND ACCUSED OF SUPPLYING GERMAN U-BOATS
IRISH AMBASSADOR CALLED TO WESTMINSTER

Mr. John W. Dulanty, Irish High Commissioner to the Court of St. James's, was handed a protest today by the English Minister of Foreign Affairs, the Rt. Hon. Viscount Halifax. It was learned that England was lodging a formal protest against Ireland for what they termed a provocative practice of succouring German undersea raiders. The note called the Irish action pro-German. It was reported early today by the Admiralty that a German U-boat was forced to the surface four hundred miles southwest of the Irish coast. When British Naval Intelligence officers boarded the German submarine, they found the entire crew in Irish sweaters. Captured German crew members would not reveal the source of their supplies. But a further search, according to British Naval officials, turned up tins of Irish oatmeal, Irish whiskey, American cigarettes, Irish glassware, silk stockings, Irish pork and beef products, and a supply of baked goods believed to be of Irish origin. Six Irish wolfhound puppies were also discovered in the sub's torpedo tubes.

It was assumed by English Naval officials that the oil in the submarine's tanks came from Ireland. Captain Herbert Browning of British Naval Intelligence, told the *Independent*, "We can only guess that Ireland has set a huge German submarine base somewhere along its coast." The British Foreign Office demanded a search of every Irish harbour and it was learned that the RAF has begun a photo reconnaissance. Several well-informed British Naval experts suggested that the Irish had built a submarine base bigger than that at St. Nazaire. "But it must be well hidden," the observer commented.

Reliable sources at the Irish Office of Foreign Affairs said that the British assumption was ridiculous. They stated that Irish communities were rural in nature and unable to support themselves, much less supply the German submarine Navy. Still it remained a mystery why the German undersea craft was laden with Irish supplies.

Some at Westminister stated that the incident was a serious one affecting the already tenuous Anglo-Irish relationship. There were speculations that Ireland had signed a secret treaty with Germany. Dr. Hemple, German Minister in Dublin was asked to comment on these allegations, but said the charges were outlandish.

"Germany can certainly supply her own U-boats, and we don't need assistance from Ireland," the minister told the *Independent*. Well-placed government sources in Dublin disclaimed any knowledge of the British charges. They said, however, that an official investigation would be undertaken.

Talk in Dublin pubs ranged from shock to laughter. One bar keep told the *Independent*, "Obviously, the British are lying again."

Another man suggested, "It seems to me—Germany has gone to the dogs .... Irish wolfhound dogs."

My hands were wet as I finished the words, and I slipped into a chair and watched Devin.

"You've done it now, Devin," Kate said. "I love it," she added with a gleeful voice.

"No business runs without a few small difficulties," he answered, patting her shoulder.

"Like bringing Ireland close to war," I said.

He did not answer but merely took off on a short stroll

around the office, feeling very good about himself, satisfied that the whole incident was a victory for his resourceful nature. Even if the truth were told to British Intelligence people, I seriously doubt whether they would have believed that an Irish boy had set up one of the most outrageous and daring schemes of the entire war.

"What are we going to do, Devin?" I asked.

"I have my plan. Obviously, the authorities will know who has been up to this trading. My name is on their lips this minute, I'll wager." (Devin was so sure of his notoriety that he wished in a sense to take full credit, though not the punishment I'm sure.)

"We must keep our heads. That's the first step. When the authorities arrive, we'll deny the whole thing. What can they do? Take a note, Billy. Number one—change the signal in Mrs. Rafferty's window. The signal has gone to red," Devin said dramatically. "Then make arrangements to unload the entire warehouse. Start hauling the goods for shipment to the Welsh ports. Next, hide all the champagne in the town. And last, but not least, I want a full scale meeting of the townspeople."

Devin called Father Dunn asking permission to use the basement of the church for an important meeting. The subject, he told Father Dunn, was a delicate matter requiring the good judgment of all the Dingle residents. But the word was out. And we did not have to instruct the people what to do; they just moved for themselves. Knitting needles were placed back into drawers and the French champagne was stored in damp and dark cellars along with the cases of French perfume. That very day, we put six vans on the road to Dublin leaving only a few pork products in the cold storage marked for shipment to England. And during that breathless afternoon, Devin hired the local sign painter to effect a message on the side of the warehouse. By five o'clock, large Gothic letters spelled out:

HELP FEED OUR ENGLAND
AND DEFEAT HITLER
Deposit all dairy and produce here for shipment to the brave people of England. God Save the King!

145

"Up the Republic!" someone yelled to a ring of laughter.

Shortly after, we walked to the church. The basement was dark and chilly, but filled with the hot, panting breath of people who had come to hear Devin and, indeed, they knew just what was to be spoken.

Devin stood on a chair at the end of the room and he began after the clapping ceased. From my position, I saw Father Dunn resting himself in the last seat. His face was blank; he was in shock.

"My friends," Devin said in the manner of President Roosevelt, "you may have heard of a certain interesting situation that has come about because of some trading we have been undertaking with a certain country which lies on the continent of Europe. Well now, as usual, the British have accused us of refueling these undersea boats and I suppose they will say next that we are making torpedoes in the cottages of Ireland and loading them in the black of night."

Already Devin had won his applause because laughter filled up the hollow spaces of the hall.

"Can you imagine the audacity of the English? They have pointed the finger at us—simple, hardworking people trying to find a place in the world and support poor, little orphans. It seems that they have taken this occasion to provoke an incident. How baking soda, Irish wolfhound puppies and beef sides could be listed as strategic implements of war I do not know. But that is the nature of the English. Next, they will be saying that we have aerodromes here and that German planes are landing in our meadows. I fully expect the English authorities from Dublin to pay us a call. And there is no reason why they should pry into our business. After all, we don't ask the Admiralty for their secrets and they're not going to learn ours. But we must all work together for the good of the nuns, for the good of Dingle and the business we have laboured to build up. I might tell you that if the English discover our ways, they might very well bomb us out and leave the town in a pile of smoking ruins.

"Therefore, we must pull ourselves together and prevent

146

this calamity. When the English come, tell them nothing. Say that we have not heard of submarines. In fact, say that we are very much on the side of the British cause. Be friendly to the British and say British things and, by all means, refer to Hitler as a dog, which he is. Our German submarine acquaintances refer to this man as a dog, so we are free to call him a filthy dog. I am certain we can be back in business as soon as this difficulty is cleared up. Thank you very much for your attention, and now we will end by all rising and singing 'The Old Soldiers Song'."

They pushed to their feet and sang out the Irish national anthem as Father Dunn dropped his head, probably more in disbelief than anything else.

TWENTY-FIVE

As clearly predicted by Devin, the British inspectors came the very next morning in a large Rolls-Royce motor car. I was looking from the office window and I saw them stop just in front. A plain-looking older man got out first—he was the Irish representative, no doubt—and he pointed to the freshly painted sign on the warehouse side. Three round-faced officials pushed their heads from the lowered windows. One was a high Naval man as indicated by the gold all over his dark blue uniform. They got out and strolled about looking at the quay, and I knew the British were saying, "Now this is a likely spot!" We realised, however, that the name Devin Ryan must have been offered as a possible candidate for submarine trade. (He was known about Dublin as something of a wild, enterprising boy from the south.) And by the degree of swiftness which brought the officials to Dingle, we knew they came to see Devin directly, rather than work their way all along the coast inspecting one harbour after another.

They entered the office and Devin moved from behind

147

his desk to greet the men. The leader, it seemed, was Captain Faraday, British Naval Intelligence, who was obviously dispatched personally to look into the matter. The other gentlemen were Embassy officials and the last inspector was someone from the Irish Ministry of Internal Affairs. After the introductions, we sat in chairs and beamed at each other. Captain Faraday was a stiff man who spoke as if he grew weeds in his mouth. His eyes were forever on Devin and I knew he suspected us straightaway.

"I noticed the sign in front," he said to Devin.

"Oh yes, we are all out for the war effort around here. By the way, how is the war going? We hardly get the news down this way," Devin asked cheerily.

"The war is going fine," the naval officer said.

"Are you down here about English food shipments? We're carrying out our share, you know."

"You are, no doubt, aware of the German U-boat which was discovered with tons of Irish goods aboard?"

"I heard about that. Now, why would the Germans want Irish dogs and silk stockings?"

"We don't know. But it's clear that these goods came from Ireland. How do you suppose they got aboard the German submarine?"

"I've been thinking that over," Devin said, moving his fingers across his brow. "And I feel that these goods came from Spain. Ireland is still trading with Spain. I believe that the U-boats were picking up these goods at Spanish ports and taking the material around to the bases in Germany."

"Interesting theory, but we think the material came directly from Ireland."

"I doubt that. Who would have the courage to load up German submarines? Why, that would be quite a risk," Devin said.

"We agree. I understand, Mr. Ryan, that you are in the hauling business."

"Yes. We haul and store goods for transport to England."

"Do you have proof of the disposition of your produce?"

148

Devin ruffled through a set of papers on his desk and came up with five sets of cargo manifests from the day before.

"Here, for instance, is a bulk of goods which went to Dublin bound for Holyhead, Wales. Beef, pork products and vegetables."

He handed over the papers and the man seemed satisfied for the time because he gave them back.

"Have you ever heard of U-boats pulling into ports along here?"

"I've never heard of such a thing," Devin said flatly. "This whole affair must be some mistake."

"We don't think so. We're going to place destroyers outside of the harbours in this area and if U-boats are coming in here, we'll finish them off in short order."

"I assure you, sir, they won't find a thing in this area. Ask anyone around Dingle."

"We'll do that."

The Englishman looked hard at my brother; there seemed to be disbelief in his eyes, a kind of helplessness too, because he could do nothing without some sort of proof. Devin took the gentlemen on a tour of the quay and a short inspection of the warehouse. Then, we all assembled at the "Bee" where the good-minded barman had hung several British war posters. The dartboard was posted with a picture of Hitler and several Dingle men stood tossing old feather darts into the black-moustached face all through our lunch of stew and Brussels sprouts.

TWENTY-SIX

Now, it was quite obvious that the British Intelligence officer looked upon my brother with a cunning, unbelieving eye. But no allegations could be thrust upon us. I think the British expected to find a vast camouflaged supply base, jammed with derricks, torpedo-loading equipment and a refueling pipe flowing with an endless supply or rich crude oil. Instead, they saw only our mock war posters and signs, none of which they tended to take seriously.

But Devin, himself, was the decoy who threw them off. And it was another brilliant testimony to his volatile, quick-thinking nature. Throughout our meal he went on repeating, "I'm only a poor country boy." To back this up, Devin dressed in his worst suit with tattered lapels and missing buttons and he pretended, if anything, to be the "Dingle dumbbell" saying such profundities as, "There's hope from the sea, but none from the grave."

"Just what do you mean by that, Mr. Ryan?" the British officer asked.

"There's fish in the sea," Devin answered with a far-off detached look.

"Yes, that's correct; there are also U-boats in the sea."

"Oh yes, undersea boats."

After a run of this sort of conversation, the party was anxious to put Dingle behind them with the greatest speed. How they ever thought they would find the guilty ones after announcing the incident in the papers, I do not know. At any rate, the sky was black during the next few days with low-flying British planes taking pictures or just flying above us as a sort of warning.

Devin, as I said, was not in the least depressed by the events; and even the further report in the *Irish Times* gave him a smile more than anything else. As I read the words, he sat in his office wearing his "thinking grin" and I knew that another, even more rhapsodic, plan was beginning to take shape on a far side of his mind.

IRELAND TURNED INSIDE OUT BY BRITISH

No U-boat bases found but allegations continue to fly

Dublin—May 20. The High Commissioner for Ireland at the Court of Saint James's, Mr. John W.

Dulanty, rejected today the note handed him by the Rt. Hon. Viscount Halifax, British Foreign Minister, late last week. It was asserted at that time by the British Admiralty that a captured German submarine was found to be loaded with Irish products including six young Irish wolfhound dogs plus a good supply of aged Irish whiskey. Mr. Dulanty stated in a note to the British Foreign Office released today: "The Government of the Irish Free State having studied the British claims of May 14th as set forth in the diplomatic note of that date, reject the allegations as false and completely unsubstantiated."

The British Navy put on display the products taken from the captured German U-boat and eyewitnesses said they were of Irish origin. The German crew refused to explain the presence of this material aboard their submarine. It could not be learned why the U-boat carried young Irish wolfhounds, but it was suspected by British Intelligence authorities that some secret mission employing the dogs was being planned by the Germans.

During the last few days, British planes have flown reconnaissance sorties over the coastal ports of Ireland hoping to discover the secret submarine base. These missions were backed up by several teams of ground inspection units from the British Naval Intelligence. When all photos were in and studied, no irregularities could be discovered. But one high-ranking British Naval authority suggested that the submarine base might be carved out of rocks on the coast of Clare, the entrance of which could be through an underwater tunnel. These charges were dismissed as being too farfetched for the Irish people to conceive without German engineering help. One comment heard in Westminster stated that Ireland maintained her position of neutrality because of a huge supply base constructed by the Germans as far back as 1936. But if this were true, the alleged base must have been better than the eyes of the schooled British agents who circulated around the Irish coast this week looking into every harbour and behind each rock in the southwest counties.

No trace of a submarine base could be discovered.

That led Irish authorities to discount the charges and state that the whole affair might have been trumped up by the Germans to wedge a serious split in the Anglo--Irish relations. High-ranking British Naval officers sent out word that they were planning to blockade remote Irish ports hoping to capture a few U-boats going in to pick up puppies and whiskey. The British Ministry in Dublin also commented that they have visited all the kennels in Ireland hoping to find the bulk purchaser of wolfhound puppies. The search finally centered on a large country house in County Cork. It was discovered that a Mrs. H. L. Mulhane had made a purchase of fifty wolfhound puppies and that she was harbouring the animals on her estate some eighteen miles from Cork. The British, in a daring nighttime raid, surrounded Mrs. Mulhane's home expecting to discover the central intelligence headquarters for a German spy and supply ring. With the aid of Irish peace officers, the English rushed the premises, firing several warning shots in the air. A servant came to the door and showed the raiding party into Mrs. Mulhane's upstairs bedroom. They found the woman to be ninety-five years of age. She was in bed surrounded by her team of young dogs. Mrs. Mulhane stated that she was filing suit against the British Ministry and the Irish Garda for invasion of privacy and entering her home without a search warrant. The British retreated after questioning the woman, who was completely unaware that a war was being waged between England and Germany.

One Irish journalist suggested that if wolfhound puppies were important to Germany's strategic battle plans, then these same dogs should be offered to the English to settle the score. All the same, dog fanciers were delighted that man's best friend was enjoying a vital role in the outcome of hostilities. Said one kennel operator in County Wicklow, "I have always thought that dogs should carry on the affairs of men. They might well make a better job of it."

Despite the remarks of dog fanciers, the British are still viewing the incident with alarm, and it is felt generally that the mysterious U-boat cargo did not bring England and Ireland closer together.

Chirps of laughter came from Devin as he listened to each word and then, as if an idea had been decided upon, he bounced up, took a deep breath and said,

"That is a shame. All the pain because of a few little hams and puppy dogs. Well, Billy, this doesn't change a thing in my mind. Restock the warehouse. We're going back into business."

"What if the inspection party comes again?" I asked.

"They won't, I assure you. Yes, stock up. We're going in for a bigger business than usual."

At that time, I had no idea what thoughts were in Devin's mind. But as so many times before, he had the certitude in his eyes and his mouth was watering money in the old familiar way.

TWENTY-SEVEN

A day later British destroyers were seen out past Dunmore Head weaving back and forth looking for submarines. Mrs. Rafferty rung up asking if she could display the green signal.

"No! No! Keep the signal red," Devin shouted into the phone. "Have you no sense?"

When our warehouse was filled again, about three days later I should say, Devin announced at dinner that his new plan was about to be put into operation. He leaned back and brought a cigar into his mouth. "We're driving to Dunmore Head. I'll say no more at this time."

Devin carried a powerful battery torch to the Rolls with

several pieces of paper. We did not speak on the way out. It was a warm night and a gentle breeze came off the sea; the heavens were painted with more stars than I had ever seen. When we arrived at Mrs. Rafferty's our light keeper was quite tipsy but luckily the red signal was still in the window. I doubt now whether any signal was necessary; certainly the Germans knowing the situation would not have dared to come close to Dingle. But I felt that they were out there someplace watching the nightly red signal. It had not failed them in the past.

Devin went over to a place in the grass and began signalling messages to sea with his torch. It was a rough international code signal, a series of dots and dashes spelling out some words in German.

"What the hell are you doing?"

"You'll see what happens," my brother said.

He flashed the signals for about an hour, then we returned to the warehouse "to wait," as Devin said. I had no idea what we were waiting for. Devin, coy as he was that night, merely lounged with his feet upon the desk reading a copy of *Fortune*. An hour later, the door flew open and Ronnie rushed in panting.

"We're being invaded! We're being invaded! A British ship just passed the harbour mouth, Mr. Ryan."

"That's fine," Devin said. "Perfect."

We followed him out to the quay and there, rounding up into the roadstead, was a four-stack British destroyer, one of those World War I derelicts which the United States awarded to the English in their hour of desperation. She came closer and we could see her mounts uncovered and swung around towards the quay. She slowed down; an Oxonian voice called from the bridge.

"Prepare to take our lines. Stand by for landing."

Her crew in helmets threw out the monkey first; we caught them and dragged the hawsers towards the mooring bits. After the destroyer was committed, the voice rang out again from the bridge.

"Oh say, how much water do you have at the quay?"

"Enough to put a carrier in here," Devin yelled back.

"Give it to me in fathoms."

"Nine fathoms at mean low water," Devin yelled.

154

The rusty grey, antiquated destroyer was secured and a rope ladder was tossed over her side to the quay. Three sailors with side-arms climbed down followed by a distinguished looking man in a duffle coat. His cheeks were bright crimson; he appeared to be either drinking or using too much make-up.

The man bowed with the grace and charm of Rex Harrison. As I saw him in the quay lights, I rather smiled to myself. He looked like a film actor portraying the venerable British Navy officer. His moustache was trimmed and red; his eyebrows were bushy.

"This is His Majesty's destroyer, *Dartwell*. I am her commanding officer, Lieutenant Commander Robert Pryce."

"Well now, I am Devin Ryan, President of the Ryan Brothers Haulage and Warehouse Company International. This is my brother, Billy, Vice-President."

"Mr. Ryan, I suppose you know of the recent U-boat incident?"

"I heard about it."

"We observed at approximately 2200 hours signals being flashed from Dunmore Head as the chart calls it. I don't know what you call it."

"We call it Dunmore Head."

"Yes. Well, my good man, these signals were read by our chief signalman. He claims they were in code. Someone here is attempting to signal U-boats. We demand the right to search the area."

Devin laughed and said, "Search no more. I was sending the signals."

"You admit it?" the English officer said with a hard, officious voice.

"About a week ago, I decided to enlist in the British Navy as a signalman. I was merely swotting up."

The British officer cleared his throat with a nervous cough. He stood looking my brother straight in the eye.

"Who did you think was going to answer you, Mr. Ryan?"

"My sending is so erratic I didn't think anyone would see it."

"Then, why did you go to the headland for your so-called practice sessions. Tell me that if you will."

"Oh, I thought, perhaps, some fishing vessel would acknowledge my signals."

Disbelief crawled all over the reddened face of the captain and small noises came from his throat.

"I demand to search the area."

"Fine," Devin said gladly. "We'll start with the warehouse."

We showed the naval man into the warehouse and he moved around carefully expecting, I suppose, a bomb to go off at any moment. His disposition was now mollified as he walked between the beef ribs.

"Here are hams, prime beef, vegetables all packed for shipment to England."

"Where in England?" the commander asked abruptly.

"You know how war is these days. These are marked for very exclusive restaurants in London and I think some cabinet officials. But that's not my business. We just supply the best meat possible."

"You know, Mr. Ryan, isn't it a shame that some people are still eating like kings. The right food, I'm afraid, goes to the wrong people."

"I don't understand."

"Look at our situation. We're here on this dreadful leaky destroyer patrolling the Atlantic winter and summer. And what do they give us? Bully-beef, the lowest grades of canned pork."

"*You* should be the ones who receive the very finest in rations . . . . like this side of prime Irish beef or this fresh vegetable. Did you ever see such a healthy beet?" Devin said, showing the rich, red vegetable and noting the aged and marbled beef sides with a sweep of his hand.

"It's all such a mistake," the officer finally said.

I remember a long and thoughtful pause which finally ended in a coughing kind of question from the commander.

"Mr. Ryan, are these supplies definitely assigned?"

"They've been ordered by a firm in Liverpool, I believe."

"And what happens if you don't fill the order?"

156

"They ring up and we tell them we're having difficulty collecting the meat because of shortages all around the south and west counties."

"Mr. Ryan, what do you get for these sides?"

"They're quite high because of the aging. You can figure about ninety percent over the market price."

"Would you, I mean to say, would you sell a few sides of beef to us in a casual sort of way?"

"Well, I don't know," Devin said with a false hesitation.

"You're feeding England anyhow. What difference would it make which British mouth takes the food? Certainly, I must say, we need it more than some fat and rich M.P. To keep our strength, you understand."

"Of course, we've always tried to do anything we could to aid the war effort; but, commander, the prices are so high."

"That's all right; that's all right," he said with a big smile tied just below his wiggling moustache.

"I might sell you a few supplies," Devin said, "just a few."

"Good. Then, it's settled."

"I hope you know the risk I am taking," Devin said.

"*We* are taking a risk, too, Mr. Ryan, needless to say."

The commander backed out of the warehouse bowing and smiling, and his mouth was already tasting the subtle flavour of the first roast beef which would be coming to the wardroom table shortly. We heard his feet patter down the quay stones in haste.

"So, that's what the plan was all about," I said.

"Of course, why do you think I was sending those messages? I knew the British patrol boats would see them and come running in here."

"But how did you know he would buy our meat?"

"Because people are people. They're not really separated by flags and international boundaries. Human nature is the same all over the world, Billy. That is the only truth I have learned."

"I do suppose that it is better that we sell just to the English."

157

"Just sell to the English?" Devin said.

"Yes."

"Billy, my dear boy, we're going to sell both sides."

"You're crazy," I yelled.

"Not in the least. If we can increase our profits, why not do it? Besides, Billy, my marriage is coming up and I want to make a quick profit so that the nuns can carry on without all these mysterious nighttime affairs. Yes, I'm sick of it. I plainly wish to settle down and lead a more normal life. My blood pressure is up."

"It'll be up plenty when the Germans come in here and find us loading English destroyers."

"Don't worry. We'll keep them apart. One week it's the Germans; and the next week it's the English."

We walked out on the quay to look at the destroyer and a high, whining woman's voice came to us over the gentle night breeze.

"Oh .... Mr. Ryan. Mr. Devin Ryan!"

We looked up at the destroyer and there was Miss Tremble leaning from one of the bow stanchions. She was dressed as a W.R.A.F. and she waved her white handkerchief in the wind.

"What are you doing up there, Miss Tremble?" Devin said.

"I'll come down and talk to you, Mr. Ryan."

Miss Tremble stepped from the gangway which had been put to our quay and she took us off into the darkness.

"I was on the destroyer, Mr. Ryan, as a food consumption adviser. I heard they were looking for the Irish sub base. . . ."

"Well, Miss Tremble, since you know the food business, from our end that is, perhaps you'll act as our unofficial agent with the British Navy."

"I would like a small share, Mr. Ryan," she giggled.

"That can be arranged."

"Are you still seeing the German U-boats?"

"Yes, as a matter of fact, business is better than ever."

"Even after that embarrassment?" she asked slyly.

Devin, with the old twinkle in his eyes, simply smiled

158

and was delighted to tell Miss Tremble about the day the British officers came into Dingle looking for the submarine base.

"Oh, Mr. Ryan, I've missed you. The letters we used to send and how we carried on here. . . ."

"Thank you, Miss Tremble. Now, we shall talk of business."

They went off towards the office and I heard Miss Tremble say, "And what about your blood pressure, Mr. Ryan? And the letters to Doctor Schweitzer and Mr. Bertrand Russell and did you remember to send the jams to Mrs. Roosevelt?"

TWENTY-EIGHT

The destroyer was loaded, the account settled, and by three in the morning she backed off our quay with Miss Tremble aboard and disappeared into the black. The following night the green signal was again posted on the Head but no U-boats came for a full week. We were having our supper one night when there was a heavy knock on the door. I opened it and standing there was a bearded man in a knit sweater and cap pulled down across his face.

"Hello, Billy," came the German-touched voice.

"God Almighty, Hans, come in."

I took the captain to the dining room where Devin jumped to his feet in a bounce of joy.

"We didn't receive word that your sub was in."

"It's not inside the harbour, Devin. We left it offshore. I used our rubber boat."

"It's good to see you. We were wondering."

"That was some predicament," he said dolefully. "Cap-

159

tain Gormitz's boat was blown to the surface, the idiot. I saw the green signal and I imagined that your brain was at work again, so I took the chance."

"Sit down and have a whiskey. A whiskey for the captain, Mrs. O'Connor."

"How does it stand?" the captain asked.

"Of course, the British are around here looking for certain undersea boats," Devin said.

"We've seen them. I can assure you, Devin, that I have held back my torpedoes."

"I appreciate that. I have excellent news. Everything is settled. The British came in last week. I have an agent aboard the lead destroyer, a person who used to work for me. We sent them up to County Clare."

"I have no doubt that some of your hams found their way aboard the British destroyer," he said slyly.

Devin hesitated a minute. I thought he would tell the truth, but he took the suggestion indignantly.

"Not that *I* know of. The destroyers won't be around here. It'll be safe now."

"How can I be sure?"

"I suppose I'll have to tell you. We *are* planning a small trade with a friend of mine on the British vessels. But I have it arranged. Two green signals and they come in; one green light and you come in. You shouldn't mind; I'm paying ten percent to keep the patrol boats off just for you, Hans."

"I'll leave you with this warning, Devin. If there's a slip or if you doublecross us, you'll be sorry. And one other thing. Those Irish wolfhounds you said were vicious. . . . I've had complaints. Two French underground intruders walked right past these so-called guard dogs at the St. Nazaire base. All they did was beg to be petted."

"I showed you how vicious they are."

"We should have kept our German shepherds. At least, they're aggressive."

"We'll refund the money."

"Now, what can I pick up tonight?"

"Meat, cigarettes, silk stockings."

"All right. The sub will be at the quay within the hour.

160

And no tricks."

"I'm an honest man," Devin said with a broad sure smile.

"Of course, you are. But I can tell you, I don't like this double trading."

"What was I to do? If I don't trade with the British, they'll wait outside the harbour and put an end to our relationship, perhaps even your submarine."

"Don't insult me. There isn't an English destroyer we couldn't pick off in a second like a wolf after sheep."

"I'm sure. Of course. But there's a price for protection. I don't like paying for protection service."

"I see the British don't care for this war any more than we do."

"No, they're sick of it."

"Pity, and it just began."

"How is the war going?" Devin asked in his usual manner.

"I'm bored by it."

"A man of your sensibilities shouldn't have to play with little ships like a child."

"I quite agree. What happened when the English came down here looking for the base?"

"They found nothing. Nothing at all. They left soon enough."

"You know that we have been ordered to stay away from Irish ports after the incident."

"I can imagine."

"I take great risk coming in here against orders."

"It'll be easy. Now, can you stay for dinner?"

"No, thank you. I wish to get on with it and clear this death trap."

"Just as safe as before," Devin said without a flutter to his voice.

Shortly afterwards, we drove the captain to a strand near Ventry where he climbed into a waiting rubber boat. The sub was brought around and once again the Ryan Brothers were back in the international trading business, wedging ham sides through the small round openings on the submarine deck.

TWENTY-NINE

The weather warmed considerably and Devin became more dreamy as early summer came to Dingle. Kate had picked a date for their marriage, and the two of them were seen ambling around the town whispering and setting great plans for the future. My brother changed once again. From a high pressure business executive, he had slipped, quite delightfully, back to the ordinary madness of a boy in love. He giggled now and then as he showed everyone in Dingle the engagement ring he had purchased for Kate. Since the future bride was an orphan herself, it was the Reverend Mother Mary Rose who took on the job of preparing Kate for the event. As I was to be the best man, my job was to hold up Devin's end.

This was a weighty assignment for two reasons. One was the fact that Devin had decided on a formal evening wedding. Two clothes-hire firms, one in Dublin and the other in Cork, joined hands to outfit almost the entire town.

The other reason for my concern in those weeks before the wedding was the sharp increase in our international trade. As the weather improved, more and more U-boats took a chance and came into Dingle. Miss Tremble had spread the word well around Falmouth because British vessels crept into the harbour with added boldness. One even arrived in the afternoon. I would say that the idea of the single and double green lanterns worked well. Mrs. Rafferty was very keen. Devin's "general store" was open to everyone without regard to race, creed, national origin or political belief (or naval affiliation). I believe that if elements from the Russian Navy had dropped in then, they might have been invited to become customers.

The Germans knew, of course, that we were trading with the English but they believed this was all arranged as a protection service. The English, on the other hand, never realised that Devin's audacity reached quite as far as it did. They thought, all except Miss Tremble who knew Devin, that whoever had been supplying the Germans had been taught a lesson.

When Father Dunn and I approached Devin on the dangers of double trading, he said, "The English would never believe we are trading with the Germans."

This was Father Dunn's first evening high nuptial mass, and the man had to swot up on the ceremony besides getting on to several deacons and sub-deacons who would assist him. Altar boys also had to be trained because, as Devin said over and over again, "I want everything to go right, Billy. Everything." The reception was to be held at the orphanage in the refectory. Devin thought that the children should take part in the affair, and so a procession was to be organised through the town with the bullet-riddled Rolls being the carriage of the bride and groom. The week before the wedding, which was to be on July 16, 1940 (alas, that date is drilled into my mind), the town began decorating. Buntings were put up, pavements and door-steps scrubbed clean, and everyone took to improving the looks of the premises. Some even were moved to bring out a paint brush and a few placed great flowers all around. It was a demonstration of love for Devin Ryan.

I could not help but think back on those days before the death of Uncle Shemas .... how Devin would come into the "Bee" with a cartoon from *The New Yorker* magazine or an article clipped from *Country Gentleman*, and everyone would simply stare at him. Some would say, "Shemas has some problem there." And yet in the passage of twenty-three months, Devin was not only taken seriously, but he was loved with a kind of special reverence. But then, my brother brought a dash to Dingle, a unity, and the people looked up to him as if he were the

163

good king who had romantically decided to take a beautiful queen from the next kingdom. It was the folklore, the myth which hangs in the minds and hearts of my people. It is not the fact but the myth which counts in Ireland and Devin took the Kerrymen from reality. That is exactly where they wished to be taken from.

The nuns made Kate's wedding dress. It was of the finest lace and they said at the orphanage that she was the prettiest bride in the world. Devin had a special morning coat made at a tailor's in Kilarney. Though the wedding was to be on the 16th day of July, it did start, in fact, three days earlier. Shops closed and there was a general party atmosphere about the town. Little business was carried on and groups stood around discussing the coming event.

"Have you heard that Mr. Ryan is planning a double-ring ceremony?"

"No, it'll be a single-ring affair."

"Could it be that the bride is nervous? That's the word. She had but one cup of tea for breakfast."

"One of the nuns said it was only toast."

(To me, it was very interesting that Dingle was discussing the breakfast habits of the bride while U-boats were loading up hams at our quay.)

The day of the wedding was bright and a deep blue was in the sky. The town literally began dressing at mid-day and everyone was so excited that few bothered to work or eat. It was the first time that many of these men had worn morning coats so the women had to help them into their hired clothes. The ceremony was scheduled to begin at half-seven in the evening and this, as I said, would be followed by a formal dinner and dancing at the orphanage. I stood before the church having a quiet cigarette and the people began to arrive a full hour before the mass.

Indeed, it was not the sort of affair which a small rural town should undertake. The men seemed awkward in their hired apparel; some wore white socks with their outfits; few suits really fitted; the cravats were sadly wrapped around many throats and were tied in many different ways. The women looked better with a slight style to their appearance.

164

Regardless of the outfits, everyone was enjoying himself. Spirits were already quite high and most of the people climbing the steps to Father Dunn's church were burping and grinning. The choir went through a heavenly sounding Latin and the organ blared better than I can ever remember, even with its off-key flat notes.

Devin stood in the sacristy quite nervous. He continued to whisper, "I'll never last."

Finally, Kate arrived in the Rolls, driven by Ronnie Downs, with Mr. Keen in the back seat who was to give the bride away. She moved up the aisle and the processional was perhaps the finest ever to be held on the Kerry coast. (There were five flower girls alone, and the altar had so many flowers that one of the deacons was taken by a coughing spell.)

The mass was going well—Father Dunn had remembered most of what he had practised—and the offertory was being sung when one of our quay hands came into the church and marched stiffly up the centre aisle to my position.

"Mr. Ryan, there's a U-boat at the dock."

This was the most shocking because Mrs. Rafferty was supposed to have changed the signal to red on the day of the wedding. (We did not wish to trade during the party.) I stepped over to her position in the church to ask the problem. This was embarrassing as everyone was looking at me. I then saw that she was asleep and there was some suggestion that she had been carrying on with the wedding celebration for some time. I moved back to my seat without too much alarm and sent the quay hand back with reassurances.

Finally, the wedding itself was performed. At the last benediction, right in the middle of the final blessing, we heard a dull explosion in the distance. Father Dunn paused and then went on. Suddenly, the quay hand dashed back into the church completely out of breath. He approached me again trembling.

"The British have arrived, sir. I believe they have a disagreement with a German vessel."

"My God!" I said.

There was another explosion and this time the windows

of the church were shaking. The nuns looked around anxiously and I finally approached the altar and whispered to Devin,

"Trouble, Devin. The British and Germans have arrived together."

Father Dunn heard me and all he said was, "I knew it. God help us now. God rest our souls."

He rattled through the last of the ceremony and said, "Go in peace." (What irony on this night.)

Grabbing Kate's hand, Devin literally dragged her down the aisle even before the recessional began. Father Dunn came right after him and then everyone jumped over the pews to reach the door of the church.

"What is the noise, Devin?" Mother Mary said.

"We have a small problem, Reverend Mother. Please take the nuns back to the orphanage . . . . just a slight argument."

Someone had already announced that the town was being attacked by the British and the nuns panicked and ran in one tight, black ball towards the waterfront. It was just about dark now and I can still see that sight of women in long formal dresses and hats with imitation cherries running down the Dingle cobbles towards the quay. Father Dunn, Devin and Kate jumped into the Rolls and we drove blaring our hooter towards the waterfront.

Indeed there was a U-boat snuggled to the quay with her deck guns pointing into the harbour towards a British destroyer, which was circling around in long lazy figures-of-eight, her five-inch guns aimed at our quay. Devin in his tails got out of the car and crossed to the Germans.

"Devin, what the hell are you dressed like that for?" Hans yelled.

"I was right in the middle of a wedding."

"Who's getting married?" Hans inquired.

"Me. This is my bride."

"I'm sorry, Devin. But war is war. I'm trapped in here now. I must do what I told you."

"Ah, what is that?"

"Destroy the town."

"Oh no . . . . no . . . . not on my wedding night."

166

"Please, sir," Father Dunn said crossing himself.

Then, the nuns came onto the quay followed by everyone in town.

"Now, Hans, I'll arrange a truce. What if I could arrange something?"

"I'll give you ten minutes, Devin," Hans yelled.

"Come on, Billy, Kate, Father," Devin ordered.

We ran towards a work boat moored to the quay; Devin and Father Dunn helped Kate down.

"My dress will be ruined for the reception, Devin."

"Kate, for God's sakes, can't you see this is the beginning of the Dingle war? Oh . . . . my blood pressure!"

"It deserves to be high right now, Devin," I added.

We threw over the dock lines, motored into the harbour and circled the destroyer.

"Is there a Miss Tremble aboard?" Devin yelled hopefully.

"There is not, sir," a voice called from the darkened bridge. "I might suggest you clear the area."

"May I come aboard? I am Devin Ryan, president of the warehouse company."

"Oh yes, Mr. Ryan, we met some weeks ago. I'm Captain Follenby. Your hams were tops, but you shouldn't trick His Majesty's Navy like this."

"There is no trick, Captain. Just a mistake," Devin said. "I want to arrange a truce."

"There shall be no compromise. We caught a German submarine in the harbour and we must set up a blockade offshore."

"You'll never get another ham from me. I'll expose you."

"No threats, Mr. Ryan, please."

"We can settle this thing," Devin said, almost shaking.

"We are planning to settle it."

"This a peaceful town. My aunt is a nun who runs the orphanage. There are children here."

On the word "children", we heard a whistle over our heads and a shell exploded just past the destroyer.

"Damn it! Hans said he wouldn't fire," Devin said.

"We'd better evacuate," Kate said, holding onto Devin.

Suddenly, both vessels opened up on each other and

167

when we had moved back to the quay, everyone was running in small panicky circles. The sub had backed off the quay and her bow was pointing towards the destroyer.

"Why the hell did Hans do this?" Devin cried out.

A salvo of shells from the destroyer hit our warehouse. A great orange ball lighted up Dingle and flames shot into the air. With a terrible thud, the whole structure came down in a pile of rubble. We ran to our Rolls as more shells continued to whistle overhead.

"What a wedding night," Kate moaned.

Our motor car was surrounded by the townspeople and there was a succession of angry shouts. It had begun raining and visibility was reduced in the harbour. But the destroyer continued to whistle shots over our heads, and one of these landed just beyond the remains of our warehouse destroying a boot shop and part of a public house next door. A deep shock came upon everyone and they stood there in the rain becoming more and more undone. Black bow ties drooped and collapsed and the women's finery became sodden. Mrs. Rafferty, quite dripping, rushed up to Devin and took him around the arm.

"It was my fault. I forgot to put up the red signal."

By this time the people believed that their town would be shelled flat and someone began an angry outburst against Devin.

"It was you who started this, Devin Ryan!"

"You and your ideas. There was peace here once."

Father Dunn ran up to the Rolls raising his hands over his head. "Listen everybody, I want everyone to listen to Devin. He will tell us what to do."

Devin climbed upon the slippery bonnet of the Rolls and he moved his wet hand across his face and tried to adjust his stiff shirt and wing collar.

"This is a crisis! We have to act! I've only tried in my heart to help this town and the nuns. I never wished to have harm come upon us. Look at my warehouse. Look what has happened."

As Devin shouted into the crowd, the German U-boat let a torpedo go, and we saw a huge flash of flame on the shore of Dunmore Head. The shot missed the destroyer by at least six hundred yards. (The only humour which came from this night was the incredible inaccuracy of the two warships. Each one could not hit the other, but their misses were destroying Dingle.)

"Here is what we will do," Devin bellowed again. His voice was sure, and something of the old Devin returned. "I have the only idea which will save us. All the women go to your homes and sit in your cupboards with the children until this thing is over and a calm brought to Dingle. Each man who has a trawler at this quay go to your vessel and crank it over. We will have to block the harbour entrance."

Devin stood there with Kate holding onto his hand and once again he raised his voice over the volley of shots, "Who's with me?"

"We are," came the unified cry.

They ran behind Devin down the quay towards their beam trawlers. In seconds, the Diesels were turned over and deep-throated sounds were heard above the rain as our fishing fleet put out into the harbour. Devin was in the lead boat along with Father, myself and Kate. We came close to the U-boat and Devin called,

"That was a bad thing you did, Hans."

"How did I know you weren't in sympathy with the British? We must protect ourselves in this war."

"Hans, in five minutes we are sinking our trawlers across the harbour mouth. Both of you and the English will be fighting a land-locked battle. When it is over, both of you will be in here to explain things to your superiors. Embarrassing to say the least. Now please carry on your dispute with the destroyer outside the harbour."

"It's another trick."

"No tricks. I am giving you the chance to be off without being tried before your Navy Board. They would court martial you for getting caught in an Irish harbour."

"That is true, Devin. I would be shot. Yes, I would be by that mad man."

"Then, you will accept the terms?"

"And how do I know the English will not lie in wait for us in deep waters?"

"You will have to trust each other. Don't you see, I'm giving each of you an honourable way out?"

"I'll agree only if the British destroyer holds her fire and comes alongside for a discussion."

(The destroyer had already ceased her fire when our line of trawlers nestled near the sub.)

Devin backed off his vessel and we motored in a long line towards the British destroyer.

"I warn you to stand clear. If you are protecting the German, we will have to destroy you," the lieutenant called down from the bridge.

"Lieutenant, in five minutes we are scuttling our fishing trawlers across the mouth of Dingle harbour. You and the Germans will be trapped in here. You can be hung for getting trapped in this harbour by a German submarine and also for trading with us illegally."

"But it is not we that are trapped. That German will never leave here."

"Nobody will leave if you persist in fighting this thing out."

Several minutes passed and the officers conferred on the bridge. Finally the lieutenant said, "What assurances do we have?"

"I've arranged a meeting with the captain of the German submarine. Pull alongside and we all may talk like men."

As the destroyer started towards the submarine, her guns still aimed at the U-boat, Devin quietly directed that all the trawlers should move towards the harbour mouth. The two vessels closed their distance, not noticing the line of trawlers which were blocking the harbour entrance, and this fact gave Devin his one trump card.

"May I introduce Captain Hans von Holburg of the German Navy," Devin called up from the deck of the trawler, "meet Captain Follenby of the Royal Navy."

"Good evening, captain."

"Good evening, captain."

"Now, it appears that a rather delicate situation has developed in this poor Irish coastal community. Both of you gentlemen are in a highly awkward and embarrassing

170

position because no one will leave this harbour."

"It is outside the harbour that we are worried about," Hans said.

"If either of you fire upon the other and do not observe the cease fire, I shall report the fact that you were trading with me in this harbour. And I have proof of it."

"I accept the terms," the British officer said respectfully. "And I suppose this means an end to our trading?"

"It does!" Devin yelled.

"I shall miss those wonderful hams," the Britisher said.

"You made the war a little easier for us, Devin," Hans said.

"But much harder on myself. I feel very tired and my blood pressure is up. Gentlemen, good luck. I am sorry this came to such an end. My warehouse is destroyed and my wedding day has come to a shambles."

Devin saluted each of the officers and we started up our trawler and returned to the quay. Both of the vessels left Dingle harbour and no warship returned, nor did we hear another shot.

That evening we walked over the rubble of the warehouse and Devin was in tears. "I tried, Billy."

"Everybody knows you did."

"Well . . . . I suppose I should be getting on with my honeymoon," said Devin. "I want you to become president of this company. I am sure we are covered by insurance and I promise that I will send on whatever money I have for Reverend Mother. I don't think I'll be back, Billy," he said in a dejected voice.

Shortly after at the orphanage, Devin and Kate entered their still war-torn Rolls, now appointed with a "Just Married" sign.

"Oh, Mr. Ryan, God bless you," Mrs. Rafferty said. "But I have a small confession to make. The Dingle war was my fault. I'm partly color blind, you see, and on some days I cannot tell red from green."

"Don't worry over it, Mrs. Rafferty. Things like that happen. Wars start for reasons much simpler than that."

"Devin, Devin," the Reverend Mother yelled over as

she came towards us, "what was all that noise down by the waterfront?"

"Nothing whatever, Reverend Mother. Just a misunderstanding. Father Dunn will explain it to you sometime."

"Goodbye, Devin," Father Dunn said, coming towards my brother. "You have been good for this town. You have imagination."

"Yes," Devin said slowly, "and look where it got me."

"Me! It got you me," Kate said.

Devin smiled, kissed his bride and climbed into the Rolls, where there was a Martini waiting for him and a box of imported cigars. He waved to us and winked, and then the Rolls went off into the night.

And that was the last anyone saw of Devin Ryan along the Kerry coast. Devin was gone forever. God bless him.

POSTSCRIPT

Devin did end up in the United States where he made great sums of money as I knew he would. Each week he sent enough to support the nuns. In 1943, I believe it was, my brother joined the American Marines and distinguished himself in the Far Pacific.

By 1945 the nuns had moved back to London and I hear there is a little plaque on the side of their new building which says, TO DEVIN H. C. RYAN WHO SAVED US DURING THE BLITZ OF 1940. GOD BLESS HIS GOOD WORK.

There is just one other significant incident which took place some years after Devin left our peninsula that should be reported. In July of 1948 a rather strange correspondence arrived at my home in Dingle addressed simply to Mr. Ryan. It was marked "Ministry of Posts and Telegraphs, Dublin". I opened it at once thinking that, perhaps, my telephone bill had lapsed. Inside the envelope was another correspondence unopened and quite yellowed by time. It caught my eye immediately as the stamp was very decorative, bearing the seal of the Vatican. The salutation from the Department of Posts and Telegraphs read, "My dear Mr. H. C. Ryan," and I knew at once that the contents were intended for my brother. I would have posted the whole lot on to him, but in 1948 all my letters to Devin were being returned from the United States with the words, "Address Unknown—Return to Sender". I read the letter knowing that I would pass the correspondence to Devin if he turned up. And it said,

My dear Devin H. C. Ryan,

As sometimes happens, letters become lost. And the Irish postal system, which has been under continual criticism from the minority leadership, is not exempt from unavoidable mistakes.

I have enclosed one such mistake. Somehow, the unopened correspondence from the Holy Father ended up behind the mirror in the gentleman's convenience at our G.P.O. in Dublin. It was brought to my attention by the new attendant, a fine man named Mr. Charlie Connelly. He said to me, 'Sir, I found this letter from the Pope. It might be important.' Of course, Mr. Ryan, I cannot apologise enough for this situation. Why the letter from the Holy Father was wedged behind the mirror in the Gent's, God only knows. I send it along to you safe, but five years late.

> Sincerely,
> Reed Donovan Esq.
> Minister, Posts and Telegraphs
> General Post Office
> Dublin

I, then, picked up the wrinkled envelope, held it up to the light hoping I could read the words without opening the letter. But the Vatican paper was of the finest quality, quite opaque, and for the first time in my life, I opened a letter not addressed to me. At the top, deeply engraved into the parchment, was the Papal Coat of Arms. The letter read:

Dear Mr. Ryan,

Your correspondence was laid before the Holy

Father and he has directed me to answer as follows:

Your good work in removing the nuns and chronically ill children from London to Dingle, Ireland, has already come to our attention and the Holy Father has remembered you in his prayers. Of course, your question about the moral crisis in your small town was, we feel, answered by yourself when you so aptly said, "There is no right or wrong in war. It is all wrong."

Therefore, His Holiness believes that your participation with the Germans shall be a matter of personal conscience. Unfortunately, we are not able to enclose money for the orphans as we are trying to support thousands of refugees in dire physical straits. The Holy Father is worried about the condition of the world, because in war it is the children and the helpless who ultimately lose no matter which side wins. It is these poor, unfortunate people, whether they be German or English, that we pray for continually.

I am happy to inform you that for your good work, His Holiness wishes to confer upon you the Knighthood of Malta. The investiture will take place at His Holiness's summer residence, Castel Gandolfo, on the tenth day of June of this year. Travel arrangements will be made through our Cardinal in Portugal.

His Holiness has also directed me to say that he wishes you to confer with several other men of good faith from the neutral countries who might be in a position to act as Papal Emissaries to bring about a permanent peace settlement.

Would you please indicate acceptance by return post.

Yours in Christ,
Alfonso Cardinale Medorini
Secretary to His Holiness
Pope Pius XII

I cannot say what effect Devin's elevation to knighthood might have had upon the Dingle War, or for that matter upon World War II. I can only shudder to think of the consequences of Devin as Papal Peace Emissary and, perhaps, it was God himself who saw to it that the Irish postal system misplaced the letter from the Holy Father.

On dark, dull nights at the "Bee", I still overhear the name of Devin Ryan being discussed. There are those who remember him well and they wish that he would come strolling back to Dingle with something new in his mind. But at any rate, Devin, wherever you are, I hope you will find this journal kind and written, as it was, with a spirit of goodwill.